She held out the cotton candy and offered it to Tate.

He shook his head in response. Cassidy shrugged, then kept on eating the sweet treat, finishing it in a matter of minutes.

He led her through the livestock enclosure as a shortcut toward getting back to the wishing tree. Cassidy paused for a moment to admire a brood of piglets running around a pen.

"You've got some cotton candy on your face," Tate said with a grin. "You always did end up wearing more of it than you ate."

His words resurrected old memories of their high school days, as well as all the church bazaars and carnivals they'd attended together. For Cassidy, it almost felt as if they'd stepped back in time to the familiar rhythms of adolescence.

This is the way we were, she thought, *before the bottom fell out of our world.*

BELLE CALHOUNE

was born and raised in Massachusetts. Some of her fondest childhood memories revolve around her four siblings and spending summers in Cape Cod. Although both her parents were in the medical field, she became an avid reader of romance novels as a teen and began dreaming of a career as an author. Shortly thereafter, she began writing her own stories. Married to her college sweetheart, she is raising two lovely daughters in Connecticut. A dog lover, she has a beautiful chocolate lab and an adorable mini poodle. After studying French for ten years and traveling extensively throughout France, she considers herself a Francophile. When she's not writing, she enjoys spending time in Cape Cod and planning her next Parisian escape. She finds writing inspirational romance to be a joyful experience that nurtures her soul. You can write to her at scalhoune@gmail.com or contact her through her website, www.bellecalhoune.com.

Reunited with the Sheriff

Belle Calhoune

Recycling programs
for this product may
not exist in your area.

 ™ LOVE INSPIRED BOOKS

ISBN-13: 978-0-373-87822-2

REUNITED WITH THE SHERIFF

www.LoveInspiredBooks.com

Printed in U.S.A.

Be kind to one another, tender-hearted, forgiving each other, just as God in Christ also has forgiven you.
—*Ephesians* 4:32

For Randy. For Everything. For Always.

Acknowledgments

A big thank-you to my daughters,
Amber and Sierra, for being so patient
and serving as my cheering squad. Many thanks
to my editor, Emily Rodmell, for her dedication
and wise counsel. And thanks to all the folks
at the Harlequin forums who help make
dreams come true, particularly Danica and Rae.

Chapter One

West Falls, Texas, Population 3,000.

Cassidy Blake read the sign as she crossed the town line into her hometown. "Who says you can't go home again?" she whispered as familiar places rolled into view.

Hunger pains began to roll like thunder through her belly. It served as a reminder that she hadn't eaten since this morning when she'd grabbed coffee and a muffin before hitting the road. At the moment a cheeseburger and fries were calling her name.

She took a quick glance at the clock on the dashboard. Was it really only three o'clock?

She'd arrived an hour earlier than anticipated. Mama and Daddy wouldn't be back home until five. She drove her car down a side street and turned back down Main so that the Falls Diner was on her left side. As if on autopilot, she pulled into the parking lot and parked her car. She drummed her nails on the steering wheel and bit her lip as she gazed out the window at the diner.

Don't be a chicken, she told herself as she took deep

calming breaths. *You have every right to sit down to a meal in the diner.* With a sigh of surrender she unfastened her seat belt and got out of the car, her legs feeling like cement blocks as she walked across the lot.

As soon as she stepped inside, the aroma of food sizzling on the griddle filled her nostrils. Cassidy looked around the room with a sense of wonder. *Nothing had changed.* The diner looked eerily similar to the way it had looked when she was a senior in high school. The leather booths were still the same pale pink color. The parquet on the floor was still black-and-white diamond shapes. The jukebox still stood in the corner, its neon colors adding life to the diner's ambiance. A smile tugged at the corner of Cassidy's lips as she remembered playing her favorite songs over and over again on it.

A young waitress with the name tag Robin pinned to her uniform came sauntering over to her. Her lips were painted a hot pink that matched her shoulder-length hair. She was chewing her gum as if it was the only morsel of food she'd be eating all day. A big smile was plastered on her face. Cassidy determined that she couldn't be any more than eighteen years old.

"Welcome to the Falls Diner. Party of one?" Robin asked in a perky voice.

"Yes, it's just me," she answered, casting a furtive glance around the diner.

Robin gestured toward the dining area. "Take whatever booth you like." When Cassidy sat down at the nearest booth, Robin placed a menu in front of her and asked, "Do you need a few minutes with the menu?"

"No," Cassidy answered with a polite smile. "I'll

have a volcano cheeseburger, curly fries and a chocolate shake."

"Sounds like you've been here before."

Cassidy nodded, deciding not to tell the waitress how many times she'd ordered that same meal. Cheeseburger, fries and chocolate shake. She'd practically lived on that meal when she was a teenager. Back then she hadn't given a thought to calories or fat content. She'd been young and carefree, filled with the knowledge that she was one of the most popular girls in town with a killer figure and a face to match.

Those were the days, she thought with a sigh. *Or had they been? Had they ever been as perfect as she'd liked to believe?*

As the daughter of the town's beloved pastor, Cassidy had been forced to rise to the high expectations of her father and the entire congregation. It had been like living in a pressure cooker, and for the first eighteen years of her life she'd done it without complaint. Perhaps it would have been better if she'd objected or rebelled, she realized. Perhaps it would have been better if she hadn't tried so hard to be Little Miss Perfect.

Cassidy shut her eyes to block out the painful memories. She chose instead to focus on one of her favorite scriptures, one that continually brought her hope and made her feel as if she wasn't so alone. *Love bears all things, believes all things, hopes all things, endures all things.*

Yes, she had sinned in the past. Yes, she had brought shame to her family. Yes, she had forever altered the life of her best friend. But did that mean she didn't deserve forgiveness? She wasn't an evil person. She hadn't willingly caused anyone pain. She'd been reckless, foolish and immature, which had been a recipe for disaster. But all that was in the past. She couldn't beat herself up anymore over it. All she could do was try and make amends.

When Robin brought her order to the table, Cassidy grabbed the cheeseburger and took a huge bite, a trickle of juice dribbling down her lips as she sent a prayer of thanks to the Lord. There was no place that made cheeseburgers like the ones at the Falls Diner. She put the cheeseburger down and reached for her chocolate shake, taking a huge sip to wash some of her meal down.

As she munched on the cheeseburger her eyes darted around the diner. Thankfully the other waitress on the floor, a woman in her early forties, was unfamiliar to her. It was only a matter of time, she knew, until she ran into one of her classmates or a member of her father's congregation. The mere thought of it made her palms moisten and her heartbeat quicken.

The diner had been the local gathering place for the cool crowd in high school, and she had been in the thick of it, holding court at a table with her best friends as if they owned the establishment. The four roses. They'd been young, beautiful and popular, with promising futures stretched out in front of them. Darkness had never touched their world, until the night the accident turned their lives upside down.

"I thought these old eyes were playing tricks on me." The gritty voice brought her out of her reverie and transported her back to a more innocent place and time.

The white-haired gentleman standing before her was Doc Sampson, the owner of the Falls Diner. He still looked the same with the exception of a few more wrinkles around his forehead and eyes. Doc had been a part of her childhood and adolescence, a man who had always been there with a jovial smile and words of encouragement.

"Doc!" she exclaimed, jumping up from her seat and wrapping her arms tightly around him. Doc hugged her back, his hands patting her on the back in a reassuring gesture.

"Cassidy! I didn't think it was possible for you to get more beautiful, but you've turned into a lovely young woman," Doc said as he broke away from the hug.

"Thanks, Doc. The years have been good to you, as well. You haven't changed a bit."

"Seeing you is really taking me back. I remember you gals used to sit in that booth over there next to the jukebox. What was it they called you girls?" He snapped his fingers as it came to him. "The four roses. That's it! You were my favorite customers. Did I ever tell you that?" His voice softened to a whisper. "Shame about what happened."

Cassidy nodded her head in agreement rather than run the risk of bawling her eyes out over Doc's kindness and sensitivity. She hadn't expected to be greeted by either in her hometown.

"Would you like to sit in that booth? For old time's sake?" Doc had a hopeful gleam in his eye, as if by seating her in the booth it might erase the events of eight years ago. *If only it were that easy,* she thought wistfully. She knew all too well the impossibility of turning back the clock.

"No thanks. I think I'll stay where I am," she said as

she sat back down in her booth. She wasn't quite ready for that walk down memory lane.

"Suit yourself, young lady." As he walked away toward the counter, he turned back to her and said, "It's nice to see you back in town. West Falls hasn't been the same without you."

"Thanks, Doc. That means a lot to me." Tears of emotion gathered in her eyes, and she sniffled a few times to rein herself in. She didn't want to surrender to a full-on sob fest. She had no desire to bring attention to herself. Although she'd known coming back home would be an emotional experience, she hadn't realized how quickly she would succumb to the flood of feelings.

The jingle of the bell heralded the arrival of another customer in the diner. She glanced up just in time to see a tall, broad-shouldered man with chocolate-brown hair step through the doorway. He was wearing a law enforcement uniform, complete with a gold badge and a cowboy hat. The nerves on the back of her neck began to prickle with awareness. Her body tensed up, while a little voice in her head urged her to run, to get away from this place as soon as possible.

But there was nowhere to run, she realized with a sinking sensation. Nowhere to hide.

Lord, give me the strength to make it past this moment.

He turned toward her and their eyes locked—she could see a hundred different emotions reflected in his. Recognition. Disbelief. Those arctic-blue eyes that she used to love gazing into now skewered her to the spot. For a moment time stood still as they took stock of each other.

"Cassidy," he said, saying her name as if it were a question.

"Afternoon, Tate," she said with a nod of her head in his direction.

She could tell just by looking at his face that she'd caught him off guard. He hadn't had time to prepare himself for seeing her. For one brief instant she'd seen a look of joy sweep over him before it was quickly replaced with one of indifference. Off guard was putting it mildly, she imagined. After all it wasn't every day that your ex-fiancée rose up to greet you like a bittersweet memory from the past.

"Mama told me you made sheriff," she said, her voice sounding stilted to her own ears. "Congratulations."

"Yup," he acknowledged with a curt nod of his head. "After Keegan retired, I was elected sheriff."

"It was always your dream, even back when we were kids. I know what it must mean to you."

"It wasn't my only dream, Cass," he said, his eyes icy and flat. "You'd know about that more than anyone."

Unable to meet his gaze, Cassidy looked down and began twirling her fingers around and around. Although she wanted nothing more than to look into those eyes and to remember what it felt like to be loved by him, she couldn't bear to see the coldness in their depths. Not when his cool blue eyes had once burned so brightly for her. Not when there was so much that remained unsaid between them, things that had been buried and lost in the aftermath of tragedy.

"What brings you back to town?" he asked with a frown.

Cassidy looked up and met his steely eyes.

"My mother has breast cancer. She's scheduled for surgery next week. I'm here to help her with her treatment and recovery."

Tate's jaw clenched, and his features tightened. "I'm real sorry to hear that. Your mama is a good woman."

"Please don't share this with anyone," she blurted out. "I mean…it's private, at least for now. Until she decides to tell everyone."

"You know me better than that, Cassidy. I won't tell a soul. That's a promise." His voice rang with conviction.

She knew better than to question Tate's word. He was as reliable as the rising sun in the morning. As far back as she could remember his word had always been bond.

"Tate, how is Holly doing?" she asked softly, the words tumbling out before she could rein them back in.

Tate's eyes widened and his face instantly hardened into a cold mask as she watched. His eyes flashed dangerously. "You've had eight years to ask that question. But you never did. You could've called, written, sent a text." Tate's lip curled upward in disgust. "But you did nothing, Cassidy. Absolutely nothing. So please, don't ask about my sister. You lost that right a long time ago."

Shame washed over her like a tidal wave, making her feel unworthy of even sitting in this booth eating a cheeseburger. It was strange, since she'd once thought she couldn't feel any deeper shame than she'd already felt. With a few scathing words, Tate had just proven her wrong.

For years she'd prayed to God to make these feelings go away, to wash away the shame so she could move forward with her life. And, for a while, she'd believed that her prayers had been answered. Until now. Until

Tate rid her of that notion with his icy blue eyes and no-nonsense talk.

"You're right," she acknowledged as pain seared through her. "I'm sorry if I made you uncomfortable."

"Uncomfortable? Is that your take on it?" Tate let out a harsh laugh and shook his head as if in disbelief. "You have yourself a nice afternoon, Cassidy."

Cassidy watched him turn his back on her and walk away. The heels of his cowboy boots tapped noisily against the floor as he made his way to the other side of the diner. Heat seared her cheeks as Doc shot her a look filled with pity. The cheeseburger turned to sawdust in her mouth, and she found it near-impossible to swallow past the huge lump in her throat. With shaking fingers she reached into her purse and pulled out a twenty dollar bill, placing it in the middle of the table where Robin couldn't help but spot it. She gave Doc a shaky wave before she hustled herself out the door and into the sultry May air. For the first time since she'd locked gazes with Tate Lynch she allowed herself to breathe—huge gulps of air that did nothing to quell the anxiety holding her in its grip.

Tate was sitting at the counter in the far left corner of the diner. His insides had churned at the thought of sitting in close proximity to Cassidy Blake. A hundred times or more he'd imagined coming face-to-face again with his ex-fiancée. None of his fantasies had come close to the stark reality. His heart had practically stopped beating the moment he'd realized that she was back in West Falls. He'd walked into the diner for his usual coffee and slice of pie, expecting to do nothing more than sit at the counter for a spell and listen to Doc's congenial chatter about the goings-on in town.

And then it had happened. *Pow.* He'd looked over and seen her at a booth, enjoying the best cheeseburger in the entire state.

She was still jaw-droppingly beautiful. West Falls High hadn't voted her prom queen for nothing. In mere seconds he'd taken it all in. The heart-shaped face. The strawberry blond hair that hung in waves past her shoulders. The sea-green eyes that always seemed to be full of mystery. Full, ruby lips. A smattering of freckles crisscrossed the bridge of her nose and extended to the landscape of her cheeks. She was all woman now, he realized. No longer the eighteen-year-old girl, fresh out of high school.

She hadn't changed much over the years, unless you counted the wary expression in her eyes that had replaced her youthful exuberance and zest for life. He supposed he couldn't blame her for being wary. Coming back to West Falls after all this time was bound to be an explosive experience, not only for Cassidy, but for everyone in town who'd been affected by her actions. Considering everything that had gone down before she'd left, she'd be dodging land mines the entire time she was here.

He quickly extinguished the burst of sympathy that flared within him at the thought of Cassidy being treated poorly. After the cruel way she had ended their engagement then fled town, he would have to be crazy to feel anything for her other than disgust. He'd once vowed never to fall for her again, and it was a vow he meant to uphold.

Holly! His sister flashed into his mind, her image serving as a brutal reminder of everything that had been broken and damaged by Cassidy's recklessness. Although he'd suffered, no one had lost more than his sister. He needed to talk to her and let her know that her former best friend was back in town. It would be cruel to let her find out about Cassidy's return from one of the town gossips or a well-meaning acquaintance. He knew all too certainly how shattering an experience it could be to be blindsided by the past.

"Don't you think you were a little hard on her?" Doc asked as he slammed down a cup of coffee in front of him, causing the inky-black contents to spill over the rim onto the counter.

Tate looked up to find Doc staring at him as if he'd stolen the cookie money from a group of Girl Scouts. His lip was curled upward and he was shaking his head from side to side.

"No harder than I should've been," Tate said gruffly before taking a long swig from his coffee mug. "Some might say she deserves a lot worse."

Doc made a loud humphing sound and plunked down a plate of cider donuts. "Well, you must feel awful proud of yourself, Sheriff Lynch. Two words from you and she went running out of here as if her tail was on fire."

"I didn't notice," Tate responded in a cool voice. *Liar,* his inner voice whispered. He'd known the moment Cassidy had left the diner. He'd seen her dart out of the place out of the corner of his eye. He'd felt an immediate shift in the diner's energy—as if all the life had been sucked out of it.

"Some might say harboring grudges isn't a healthy

way to live one's life," Doc grumbled as he wiped up the spilled coffee from the counter.

Tate let out the breath he'd been holding ever since he'd laid eyes on the only woman he'd ever loved. It did nothing to ease the tightness in his chest. "Can't help it, Doc. Not a thing has changed since she left. My sister's still in a wheelchair. She's still paralyzed from the waist down. I'm not about to pretend as if all is forgiven."

Doc's face softened, and all the harshness went out of his voice. "What happened to Holly was devastating, Tate. Not just for your family, but for the whole town. The Blakes included. Why is it so hard for you to see that Cassidy has suffered also?"

Tate clenched his jaw in response to Doc's words. It didn't sit well with him that Doc was portraying Cassidy as the victim. He forced himself to count to ten before he blasted his old friend. He had to remind himself that Doc wasn't the enemy. It wasn't Doc who'd kept him up nights tossing and turning. It wasn't Doc who'd broken his heart and shattered his faith in love everlasting. No, that honor went to his high school sweetheart, Cassidy.

"It's not my problem," he said with a hard edge to his voice. "She made her choice years ago when she took off. She left my sister without a word of goodbye, without even a word of apology. What kind of person does that?"

Doc shook his head and sighed. "Just ask yourself what you're really angry about, son. Is it because of the accident or is it because she left you two months before you were supposed to get married?"

Tate pulled out his wallet and plunked down a few bills on the counter before getting up from his stool and grabbing a few cider donuts to bring back to the sheriff's office. Although he was annoyed at Doc for defending Cassidy, he wasn't about to let his favorite snack go to waste. He knew if he stayed here any longer he would be in jeopardy of losing his temper and violating the very code that made him such a well-respected lawman.

"Thanks for the coffee." Tate walked out of the diner with long powerful strides that carried him quickly to the parking lot where his squad car was parked. As he revved the engine, Doc's words rang in his ears like a haunting melody. *Just ask yourself what you're really angry about.*

He wasn't used to anyone questioning his resentment toward Cassidy. For so long these feelings had festered inside of him, stoked by the bitter sentiments of his family members and the negative opinions of the townsfolk. Was Doc right in questioning his motives? Was his inability to forgive Cassidy more about his wounded pride than anything else?

Although his feelings were too jumbled to process at the moment, there was one cold hard truth he found impossible to deny. When he'd first laid eyes on Cassidy in the diner, he'd fought against a powerful yearning to pull her into his arms and welcome her back home. Try as he might, he couldn't stop remembering how good it felt to love and be loved by Cassidy Blake.

Chapter Two

You lost that right a long time ago.

Try as she might, Cassidy couldn't get Tate's words out of her head. Her confidence had been shaken by their run-in. As she maneuvered her light blue Honda through the center of town she adjusted her speed to meet the thirty-mile-an-hour speed limit. As a teenager she'd routinely ignored the sign, putting the pedal to the metal as she rocked out to the latest chart-topping hits. Back then her car had always been filled with a group of girls, the best friends she'd thought she'd have in her life forever.

They'd been in each other's pockets all through junior high and high school. Holly. Jenna. Regina. And Cassidy. Until the tragic night that had changed everything in their lives, destroying their friendship and turning them into bitter enemies. Although they'd made a pact never to reveal the circumstances of the crash, their friendship had come apart under the strain. And she'd taken all the blame for the accident, she thought with a tinge of bitterness, even though all four had participated in a reckless game of chicken.

She gave in to a smile as familiar places rose up to greet her—the town library, Lucky's Bowlarama, Daisy's Hair Salon. There were new establishments, too—a candy store called Sweet Tooths and a doggy spa called Bow Wows.

As she drove down Main Street a sense of happiness went straight through her, despite the knot resting in the pit of her stomach. The feeling of joy surprised her, stunned her even. For eight years she'd avoided West Falls like the plague, her heart filled with the knowledge that she would be as welcome in her hometown as a raging Category 5 hurricane.

But circumstances had given her no choice in the matter. The one person she couldn't say no to had asked her to come back home. And so, for the next few months, she was back in West Falls to tend to her mother and to face up to her past. It was the least she could do for the one person who'd always had her back and still regularly told her she loved her.

As she came to the intersection of Oak and Main, her foot slammed down hard on the brake. She looked out of the passenger-side window and let out a deep sigh as she laid eyes on her father's church. She pulled the car over so that she was parked directly in front of Main Street Church. She'd spent half of her life in this place of worship, attending Bible classes, singing in the church choir and sitting in the first pew to listen to her father's Sunday sermons. It was still an imposing structure, still beautiful with its vibrant stained glass windows, soaring steeple and elaborate stonework that must have been a recent addition.

Main Street Church. Her home away from home.

How she missed being a member of this congregation. There was a huge void in her life that the church had filled up when she was a member. That sense of family and community had been as elusive as a will-o'-the-wisp in Phoenix. Tears misted in her eyes as she remembered all the church socials and outings she'd attended during her years in West Falls. The congregation at Main Street Church had been like extended members of her family, most of whom she'd known since she was a baby.

But, like everything else good in her life, she'd lost it all due to one moment of recklessness.

She could almost hear her father's voice quoting Proverbs—*The wise will inherit honor, but fools get disgrace.* She winced at the memory of her father's fury after the accident. If she lived to be a hundred she'd never forget the scathing words he'd hurled at her like an explosive grenade. *Disgrace. Shame. Disappointment.*

Those words were now embedded in her heart like a permanent tattoo.

After her run-in with Tate, Cassidy knew she should make her way to her parents' house before word of her arrival in town began to circulate in the gossip mill. She knew from past experience how quickly news traveled in a small town like West Falls. But when she tried to start the car, the Honda made a sputtering sound, then came to a shuddering stop.

"What in the world?" Cassidy asked as she tried to start the car up again. The engine made a whirring sound as she revved it, but it didn't start.

She looked at the fuel gauge. There was still gas in the tank. Frustration poured through her as she realized she was dealing with a mechanical issue. She'd made it all the way from Phoenix, only to break down in the center of town, mere blocks from home.

Was God trying to tell her something? Of all the places for her car to break down, why did it have to be in front of Main Street Church? Why did it have to happen on her first day back in town? She stepped out of the car, slamming the door behind her as her mind raced with ideas about how to get out of this predicament. She didn't have the slightest clue as to who to call to service her car. Although she vaguely remembered an auto body shop in town, she couldn't recall the name of it.

She looked up and down Main Street, her eyes honing in on an approaching police car. Cassidy watched as the squad car slowed down and made a left onto Oak in front of the church.

"Oh, Lord. Please don't let it be him," she prayed. "Anyone but him."

The run-in with Tate was still fresh in her mind. She'd been stung earlier by his surly attitude and comments about Holly. While a part of her didn't blame him for hating her, another part of her ached to see him look at her with an emotion other than disgust.

As the squad car came to a stop behind her car, she watched as a familiar pair of broad shoulders stepped from the car. Tate was staring straight at her, his blue eyes like laser beams as he assessed the situation. The sight of him striding toward her caused her pulse to quicken and beads of moisture to pool on her palms.

"Oh, come on," she muttered. "Can this actually be happening to me?"

His long powerful legs brought him to her side in a few quick strides.

"Car trouble?" he asked, his voice brisk and businesslike.

She let out a deep sigh. "I don't know what happened. I took my car to the shop two weeks ago for a checkup." She threw her hands in the air. "I've traveled all this way, only to conk out in the final stretch."

Tears pricked her eyes, and she blinked them away. She didn't want to be weak in front of Tate; she didn't like feeling helpless. It reminded her way too much of the past and the way she used to feel. She'd worked extremely hard in her life to move past those feelings of helplessness. But with her mother's illness, her long-overdue return to town and the sudden breakdown of her car, her vulnerabilities were rising to the surface.

Tate reached out and rested his hand on her shoulder, his touch shooting warmth through her entire body. "It's okay, Cassidy. Just take a deep breath."

Just take a deep breath. He'd said those familiar words to her a hundred times or more during their relationship. Whenever she'd been stressed or high strung, he'd uttered those five words as a means of calming her down. And it had always worked, Cassidy realized. She closed her eyes and took a deep breath, reminding herself that this difficult moment would soon pass.

When she opened her eyes he was still standing there, his gorgeous face filled with concern.

"I have Lou's shop on my auto dial. We'll have them come pick up your car, and I'll drop you off at your parents' house." The lines of his face had softened, and for a moment she could almost pretend as if nothing had changed between them. He looked so much like the Tate who'd loved her. She had to resist the impulse to reach out and touch his face. It was something she ached to do, but knew she had no right to.

She clenched her hands at her sides. "You don't have to do that," she protested. "I can call a cab or something."

The last thing she wanted to be was a burden to him. He'd made it perfectly clear at the diner that he wanted nothing to do with her. Even though he was town Sheriff, under the circumstances it would still be above and beyond the call of duty to come riding to her rescue.

He frowned at her. "I know I don't have to, Cassidy. I'm law enforcement in this town. I'm not about to leave you stranded out here." His lips curved upward in the slightest of smiles. "And in case you don't remember, West Falls only has one cab, so you might be waiting out here for quite a spell."

Cassidy laughed. "I guess I forgot about that." She looked up at him, warmth filling her insides at his sudden playfulness. *How she missed this.*

He folded his arms across his chest and stared her down. "So, what'll it be? A ride in the squad car or waiting in the hot sun for an elusive cab ride?"

Not much of a choice, she realized. Although riding with Tate would be awkward, it was the most convenient option at hand. She couldn't run away every time she ran into him. It was bound to happen throughout the course of the summer, particularly in a town the size of West Falls. She needed to compose herself and act like a grown woman, not like the teenaged girl who'd been head over heels in love with Tate. That might work, she thought, if she could only tell her heart to stop slamming inside her chest every time he was nearby.

"I accept the offer. It's mighty kind of you." Kindness. It was Tate's signature, as much a part of him as the cleft in his chin. And even though his actions were well-meaning, she couldn't imagine a worse torture than being physically close to him, but separated by a world of differences.

Tate nodded curtly and pulled out his cell phone to contact Lou. When she pulled her suitcase from the trunk of the car, she felt strong hands taking the luggage from her grip. Without a word Tate swept up all her bags and carried them over to his car, depositing them in the backseat. She followed behind him, sliding in on the passenger side.

When Tate seated himself behind the wheel, he glanced over at her. "Someone will be here within five minutes to tow the car to the shop. You'll need to call them later with all your information. They'll probably have an estimate for you by then."

Cassidy murmured her thanks, appreciation flowing through her at how easily Tate had fixed things. A few minutes ago her problems had seemed overwhelming. Although she considered herself an independent woman, it was a nice feeling to have someone to lean on. *That's what she'd been missing since she'd left West Falls. Someone to lean on.* There had been several boyfriends in her life in the past few years, but not a single one had ever touched her heart the way Tate had. Not one had ever made her feel as if he'd been the other half of her soul.

Tate reached over and placed his cowboy hat on the

dashboard, his arm brushing against hers in the process. She sucked in a short breath, her nerve endings tingling at the sudden contact. The spicy, woodsy scent of his aftershave rose to her nostrils, bringing back memories of being held tightly in his arms and inhaling that intoxicating scent.

For a few moments the only sound inside the car was the low hum of the squad car radio as it crackled and buzzed. A slight tension thrummed in the air. She was all too aware of her close proximity to Tate and his each and every move as he maneuvered the car. His right hand gripped the steering wheel while his left arm rested on the windowsill. Every now and then he would tap his fingers against the wheel, moving to a beat only he could hear.

Tate cleared his throat. "I hear you have a gallery in Phoenix." He cast a quick glance in her direction. "I was a bit surprised at that. You always said you wanted to teach art to children. That didn't work out?"

Had Tate kept up with the goings-on in her life? She'd only had her gallery for two years, so clearly someone had filled him in on her news. Did he actually care about her life or was he simply filling the time with small talk?

She shrugged. "I was an assistant to a gallery owner when I first moved to Phoenix, so I spent years learning the ins and outs of how to successfully run a gallery. It was the next logical step for me to run my own."

She stole a quick look at him, curious to gauge his reaction.

"Logical? Since when has art been logical? You used to say it was primal."

Silence hovered in the air between them. She wasn't sure how to respond to Tate's question. Or had it been a dig? Was he making some negative statement about her career? Or was she being paranoid? At the moment she couldn't even think straight. Being in such close confines with him was doing strange things to her insides. Her heart was beating a fast rhythm within her chest while butterflies were fluttering in her belly.

"You're right. My relationship to art is very primal. I suppose over the years I've learned to be more practical about it. It's a business after all." She'd learned that lesson shortly after graduating from art school and searching for an art position that would provide her with a decent income. Although it had been her dream to work with children, circumstances had forced her to alter that dream in order to keep a roof over her head. But that dream had never died. It still lingered in her heart.

"As long as you're happy," he responded in a low voice.

Happy? It had been a long time since she'd considered her own happiness. Did her life in Phoenix bring her joy? Yes, at times it did. She had her gallery, a group of close friends, loyal patrons and her artwork. But there was still a gaping void in her life she'd never been able to fill.

She turned toward him, admiring the strong tilt of his jaw and the masculine beauty of his face in profile. There was so much she wanted to tell him about her life and the path she'd been walking on for the past eight years. But the gap between them was too wide. They no longer had the type of relationship where such intimacies were shared.

"I still want to teach kids how to paint," she explained, her voice sounding defensive to her own ears. "I just haven't put the pieces together and figured out how to make that happen."

"You will." The simplicity of his words touched her in a place that hadn't been breached in a very long time. He believed in her. Still, after everything that had come to pass between them. She felt a pang of longing so sharp it almost made her cry out. *This is why she'd loved him. This is why she'd known at eighteen years old that she wanted to spend the rest of her life with him. This is why she still hadn't been able to forget him and move past what they'd shared.*

She shifted her body away from him and stared out the window, willing away the tears that she was holding at bay.

As Tate drove down Magnolia Drive, the street she grew up on, a feeling of nostalgia swept over her. So many memories were created on this very street—setting up lemonade stands with Regina and Jenna, selling Girl Scout cookies door to door with Holly and riding her bicycle with the neighborhood kids until night crept in and stamped out the sun. The street was still as impeccable as ever. A few things have changed, she realized, as she spotted a twentysomething couple pushing a stroller, as well as new construction under way on an older ranch-style home.

Tate came to a stop in front of her parents' house. She let out a sharp intake of breath as she laid eyes on her childhood home. The white Victorian with the wraparound porch and the sea blue shutters looked exactly the same as when she'd left West Falls.

"Are you okay?" Tate reached out and placed his hand on hers. "It's been a while since you've been back home. You're bound to feel some kind of way about it." His voice had softened, and although she longed to lean into his strong shoulders and rest her head there, she knew those days were over.

"It's a little overwhelming," she admitted. "But I feel fine. This is going to sound crazy, but it almost feels as if time stood still while I've been gone. I suppose that's the beauty of having a place to call home. It seems like it was just yesterday that I was here, running out the front door to meet up with you or scrambling to get to school on time. I can't believe it's been so long." She did her best to keep her voice steady and calm as the memories washed over her. Tears pooled in her eyes as she gazed at the place where she'd grown up. *Home.*

"Eight years is a long time, Cass. Give yourself a chance to soak it all in." His words were warm and encouraging, serving as a memory of everything she'd left behind. *Hearth and home. The people who loved her. The life she could have had with Tate.*

As she stepped from the car, Cassidy's eyes were drawn to the maple tree—it was still standing in the side yard, majestic and strong. A strong memory tugged at her—climbing up this tree with Regina and Holly while Jenna stood on the ground and watched. It had always been her father's favorite tree, while her mother had favored the birch tree in the back yard. A few flowers were in full bloom in the garden on the side of the house—vibrant bluebells and white roses.

Tate pulled her luggage from the car and deposited

it next to the walkway. He walked over and joined her in the side yard where she was admiring the garden.

"You know, I used to think you had the perfect life. Your father was the pastor of the biggest church in town. Your Mama was so devoted to your family. She reminded me of one of those perfect TV moms. And you…" His voice hitched a little and a wistful look settled on his face. "You were everything. Cheerleader. Prettiest girl in town. Prom queen. Beloved by all."

Cassidy shook her head, lightly fingering one of the roses. "It was never perfect. I know it may have looked that way, but there were a lot of cracks in the veneer. And then those cracks turned into major fissures." She let out a huff of air. "Being the pastor's daughter was exhausting. I loved being a member of the congregation, but everyone in town expected so much from me, including my father. There was so much pressure to be perfect. I had to wear the right thing, say the right thing, do the right thing. And when I fell from my pedestal…." Her voice got small and a tightness seized her chest as the painful memories washed over her. "Well, I fell pretty hard. I was the town pariah."

Cassidy looked up at Tate, and their gazes locked. He clenched his jaw tightly, his eyes swirling with turbulent emotions. A heaviness lingered in the air between them.

"You should consider yourself fortunate that we didn't get married. I doubt you would've made sheriff if you'd been married to me." She tossed the words out in a flippant tone, desperate to mask the hurt and pain that he'd uncovered.

The hurt and pain, she'd long ago realized, was always there hovering beneath the surface, waiting to rise up at moments like this.

Tate's expression turned dark, and he gritted his teeth. "Like I said before, becoming Sheriff wasn't my only dream." He took a step closer to her. "And for the record, I've never considered it a blessing that you didn't want to marry me."

Her eyes widened. "Tate! It wasn't—"

The sound of a slamming car door interrupted them and drew their attention to a dark stylish vehicle parked in front of her parents' house. For a brief moment she wondered if someone had stopped by after hearing of her return to town. She began to bite her lower lip. Perhaps it was someone who wanted to yell at her. She squared her shoulders, lifted her chin a few inches higher and prepared herself for battle.

Lord, give me the grace and courage to greet my enemies with a smile.

A tall, broad-shouldered woman dressed in a red sundress came into view, a big bouquet of flowers cradled in her arms. With her brunette pixie hairstyle and round face, she was instantly recognizable from where Cassidy stood in the driveway. Although it had been years since she'd seen her cousin Regina, a sense of familiarity swept over her at the sight.

"This day just keeps getting better and better," Cassidy muttered.

Tate raised an eyebrow. "I think I should stick around for this." He edged a little closer to her so that their elbows were touching.

Regina took off her sunglasses and squinted in their direction. "Cassidy? Is that you?"

"Hi, Regina. It's nice to see you."

"Regina." Tate tipped his cowboy hat in her direction. "How are things?"

Regina walked toward them with her mouth hanging open. As always, she tended to be on the dramatic side. "What are you doing here, Cassidy?" Her eyes pivoted to Tate. "And why is Tate here?"

Well, hello to you too, cousin. She didn't quite know what to make of her cousin's blunt questions. Why hadn't her parents told Regina she was coming home? Years ago they'd hung out in the same social circle and had been the best of friends. Occasionally they'd struggled with petty jealousies and rivalries. But they'd been close, whispering secrets in Cassidy's bedroom well after her mother called for lights out. Now Regina was staring at her as if she was as unwelcome as a raging thunderstorm on a summer's day.

She took a deep breath, reminding herself that Regina sometimes had a gruff approach that hid a softer, more vulnerable side.

"I'm here to be with my mother," she explained in a calm voice.

"Does she know you're coming?" Regina asked.

"Of course she does. She asked me to come home," she answered. Regina's comments were making her feel like an outsider.

Regina's eyes widened. "She did?"

"Yes, I am her daughter after all. Who better to nurse her back to health than me?"

"Enough with all the questions," Tate said pointedly, his eyes flashing warning signs. "Cassidy's had a long day that ended with her car breaking down over by the church. You can save the interrogation for later."

Relief swept through her, and she shot him a look of gratitude. Dealing with her cousin wasn't always easy. Somehow Tate had always possessed a knack for being able to handle her.

Regina turned to Tate, her eyes filled with remorse. Her voice softened. "I'm sorry. I was just so surprised to see the two of you together after all this time. I had no idea Cassidy was coming back to town, so it was a little jarring running into her out of the blue like that."

Cassidy sighed. "My car broke down right outside Main Street Church. Thankfully Tate drove by a few minutes later. He called the auto shop and gave me a ride over here."

Regina grinned. "That's our sheriff. Always riding to the rescue."

Cassidy didn't miss the way Regina leaned toward Tate and playfully jabbed him with her elbow. She felt a twinge of irritation. *Some things never change.* Regina had always been a little bit of a flirt. She wasn't proud of it, but she'd always been a tad jealous of the playful interaction between the two of them back in the day. A tightness constricted her chest as the realization hit her that Tate and Regina might have connected over the years, perhaps even dated. It wasn't as if her mother ever mentioned Tate's love life in any of her phone calls or emails since Cassidy had told her long ago that he was a taboo topic of conversation. The sole exception had been when her mother had given her the news that Tate was the new town sheriff.

Regina and Tate? No, Cassidy told herself. Tate

wouldn't do that to her. He knew that she and Regina loved each other despite their ups and downs. He wouldn't betray her like that with her own cousin. *Or would he?* He'd been so angry with her when she'd called off their wedding. Although she'd tried to explain herself to him, he hadn't wanted to hear a word of it. She remembered vividly their last moments together. When she'd ended things, Tate had slammed his fist into the barn door of his family's ranch. His hand had been bruised and bloodied. It was the first time since she'd known him that his actions had frightened her. The look of intense anger in his eyes had chilled her to the bone and left her quaking with unsettled emotions. Love, fear, guilt. It had been so confusing dealing with all her jumbled feelings, so much so that all she'd wanted to do was leave town and all her troubles behind her in the rearview mirror.

And in doing so, she'd earned herself a permanent place in West Falls's hall of shame.

"Tate driving by at that exact moment was a godsend," she replied in a calm, even tone. "I don't know what I would've done if he hadn't driven by."

Regina's eyes twinkled. "Well, you know what they say. God works in mysterious ways." Regina was smiling and looking back and forth between them. She was trying to insinuate that God had placed the two of them together for a reason.

Tate was shooting daggers at Regina. Clearly he hadn't missed her innuendo and wanted nothing to do with it. Heat burned her cheeks as she turned her gaze away from Tate. It had been ages since she'd felt so embarrassed. She sent her cousin a pointed look. She wasn't in the mood for Regina's matchmaking. Did she seriously think that they could just walk back into each other's arms after all this time? Didn't she realize that the truth about the accident stood between them like a wedge?

The sound of a car crunching on the pebbled driveway caused them to turn away from each other and focus instead on the gray sedan idling in the driveway. With her heart in her throat Cassidy watched her father exit the car and scramble around to the passenger side, where he opened the door and gingerly pulled her mother from the car. Her mother, dressed in light blue slacks and a short sleeved polo shirt, leaned on her father's arm and walked with measured steps.

The sight of her mother walking toward her pulled at Cassidy's heartstrings in a way that nothing else could. She was thin, she realized, so much thinner than she'd ever seen her. The color in her face was unlike her usual healthy complexion. She looked sallow and worn out. Although her father had warned her about what to expect due to the chemotherapy treatments, nothing could have prepared her for the sight of her ailing mother.

Maylene Blake had always been a beautiful woman, and she still maintained traces of that beauty, despite the illness ravaging her body. With auburn hair that fell around her shoulders, emerald-green eyes, bow shaped ruby lips and a pair of dimples that would make the angels cry, Maylene had been a Miss Texas and competed in the pageant circuit. She was wearing a wig, Cassidy noted, no doubt to mask her thinning hair and bald patches. Although her lips had lost a little color, her eyes still lit up like the bulbs on a Christmas tree as soon as she spotted Cassidy.

"Cassidy!" her mother cried out. "You're here. Oh, the Lord is good to me."

Cassidy took two long strides and quickly reached her mother's side. With all the tenderness she possessed, she pulled her mother into an embrace. Her mother kissed her on the cheek and murmured thanks to the Lord for bringing her back home. The scent of her mother's Chanel No. 5 perfume rose to her nostrils and hurtled her straight back to childhood when she'd played dress up in her mother's closet and spritzed herself with enough of the scent to last a lifetime. She couldn't help but feel her mother's rail thin body through her shirt when she wrapped her arms around her. If nothing else, she was determined to cook for her mother and put some meat back on her bones.

She watched as Tate leaned down and planted a kiss on her mother's cheek, then turned to shake her father's hand. Genuine warmth flared between them. Her mother's eyes twinkled as she gazed upon the man who'd been slated to be her son-in-law.

"I'm going to leave you all to your reunion," Tate drawled, with a polite nod in her parents' direction.

"Please come inside for some lemonade before you leave. It's mighty hot out here," Maylene suggested, her face lit up with a warm smile.

"No, Ma'am. Thanks for the offer, but I've been away from the Sheriff's Office for a while now. I need to get back and check on things." Tate's firm tone brooked no argument.

"Thanks for the rescue. And the ride." Cassidy forced

herself to smile, despite the lead weight lodged in her gut. He was leaving! She wanted him to stay, to come into the house and sip lemonade with her family. More than anything, she wanted him to smile at her again, to joke with her about trivial matters and tell her his innermost thoughts. A strong force tugged at her. She wanted things to be the way they used to be.

Tate nodded curtly, his expression unreadable as he turned and walked away, his stride full of purpose.

He can't get out of here fast enough! Her heart sank as the realization kicked in. Tate was rushing away as if his pants were on fire. Any illusions she'd been harboring about him wanting to spend time with her vanished as she watched him speed away. What did she expect? A kind deed and a few civil words didn't change Tate's feelings toward her. She'd seen it all in his eyes—the mistrust, the pain, the regret.

As Regina rushed ahead to open up the house, her father linked her mother's hand with his and began walking toward the door with her. Cassidy positioned herself on her mother's right side, supporting her as she walked up the steps and onto the porch. Cassidy cast a glance backward, only to see the squad car turn off the lane and zoom out of sight.

Once inside Regina began running around fluffing up pillows, bringing bottled water and a stack of magazines to read. Cassidy watched Regina flit around the house with an ease that she envied. She battled a rising sense of irritation as her cousin played the role of doting daughter while she stood on the sidelines.

Lord, please help me to deal with these feelings of resentment. I shouldn't be jealous of my cousin's close-

*ness to my parents. I should be grateful that she's cared
for them in my absence.*

Gratitude was the last thing she felt as Regina
clapped her hands together and cried out, "Why don't
we do one of our puzzles, Aunt Mylie? I can run to your
sitting room and bring down a few."

Her father gently pulled his niece aside and began
talking to her in hushed tones, his expression earnest.
Regina's eyes widened and a look of dismay came over
her face. Cassidy heard her cousin murmur, "I... Oh, of
course. I really just stopped by to see how Aunt Mylie
was doing. I'm sure you want to spend some quality
time together."

Regina spun around and grabbed her purse off the
end table. "I'm going to go do a food run," she said
briskly. She looked at her watch. "I should get going
before the shops close."

"I'll walk you to the door, sweetheart," Maylene said
as she patted Regina reassuringly on the back.

Regina walked over to Cassidy, wrapping her arms
around her once she'd reached her side. Cassidy felt her
body relax as she gave in to the rush of warm feelings.
This was home. "I forgot to say welcome back, Cassidy," Regina whispered. "I've missed you."

"I missed you too," Cassidy said in an earnest voice.
And she had missed her. Terribly.

Although her relationship with her cousin wasn't
perfect, it was based on deep love and abiding family
values. Reconnecting with Regina while she was back
in town was at the top of her to-do list.

"I'll come by later with dinner," Regina called out
as she breezed out of the room.

As soon as they were alone in the living room, her father turned toward her, his eyes inscrutable as he gave her the once-over. With his salt-and-pepper hair, slate gray eyes and tall thin frame, he cut an imposing figure. Ever since she was a little girl, Cassidy had been both in awe of and afraid of her father. At twenty-six years old, she found that nothing had changed in that regard—her knees were shaking and her palms were slick with moisture.

Lord, help me bridge this gap between us. We're miles apart and every day the gap gets wider.

"Cassidy. It's been a while," her father said stiffly, his arms lying helplessly at his sides. Just this once she wanted him to wrap those long arms around her, to take away all the pain and fear filling up her insides. "It's good to see you back home."

"It's good to see you too, Daddy."

She threw herself against her father's chest, giving in to a wild desire to hug the man who'd given her life. It had been so long since she'd been embraced by him. She inhaled deeply, savoring the woodsy natural scent that took her all the way back to childhood. She wrapped her arms around her father's waist, waiting to feel his loving embrace, his tender show of affection. Before she was ready to let go, she found herself being gently pushed away from him.

"You look well, Cass. I'm happy you came back to help your mother," he said gruffly, his expression blank. "She needs you."

"There's no place I'd rather be," she said. "I didn't realize how much I missed West Falls until I got here."

"And your work? I hear your gallery is doing well."

"Yes, quite well," she said proudly. "You remember my assistant, Anna? She's agreed to run the gallery for me so I can stay here for the summer. Longer, if Mom needs me."

"And that young man we met the last time we were in Phoenix? Roger, wasn't it?"

Her heart sank. "We broke up a few months ago. I wasn't ready for anything serious."

Her father opened his mouth to say something and then closed it. For a moment she could see a glimmer of emotion in his eyes. As quickly as she noticed it, the look was gone, replaced by a shuttered expression.

"Well, I'd better go write my sermon for Sunday's service. Time waits for no man. And these days the congregation needs inspiration more than ever."

An emptiness seized her as she watched her father walk away from her and down the hall to his study. To Cassidy it felt like he couldn't get away from her fast enough. Just like Tate.

Yes, Daddy, she wanted to shout out. Your congregation may need you, but so do I. I always have. Why can't you see that?

Tears streamed down her cheeks as cold, hard reality hit her square in the face. Even though she'd prayed on it for the past eight years, in the eyes of her father she still remained unforgiven. He always preached about the Lord's forgiveness—for adulterers, liars, thieves, murderers—but not for his only child, the one he should put above all others. Didn't he realize she'd already paid the ultimate price by giving up everything that mattered when she'd left home?

* * *

"Sheriff Lynch?"

Tate jumped to attention as the voice of his deputy Cullen Brand drew him out of his reverie. He'd been sitting in his office gazing out the window, his thoughts centered around a gorgeous woman who'd owned his heart for as long as he could remember. No matter how far Cassidy had roamed from West Falls, he'd always considered her a part of the landscape. His hometown had never been the same without her. His heart had never been whole.

She looked every bit as beautiful as when she was crowned prom queen. Even more beautiful if he was being honest with himself. If he closed his eyes he could recall the exact shade of dress she'd worn that evening—lilac. With the rhinestone tiara on her head, a pair of dangling earrings and the strappy silver heels, she'd looked like a fairy-tale princess come to life. And he had been her Prince, her forever. Pain speared through him at the memory of all they'd been—happy, golden, innocent.

His love for Cassidy had been epic, the stuff of which dreams were made, and he'd believed they would go the distance and grow old together. He couldn't have been more mistaken.

Stupid, romantic fool.

Thoughts of Cassidy dominated his mind, making it difficult to focus on work. Coming face-to-face with her after so many years had thrown him for a loop. He found himself replaying their conversation over and over again in his head. Had Doc been right? Had he been too hard on Cassidy at the diner? He'd battled

a host of emotions this afternoon—anger, joy, bitterness, mistrust—so much so that by the time he'd left
the Blakes' home he'd been in a tailspin. Being at their
house had been like taking a nostalgic walk down memory lane. It brought back bittersweet memories.

"What is it, Cullen?" he asked as he sat back in his
chair and took the opportunity to give Deputy Brand
the once-over. Cullen was a fine addition to the Sheriff's Office, he reckoned. He was considered husband
material by the ladies in town who seemed to have a
fondness for his curly dark hair and laid-back approach.
He stood five feet eleven inches tall with a leanly-mus-
cled build and a sweet smile women found endearing.

Cullen was a good guy and an even better deputy, if
a bit of an enigma. He was standing two feet away from
Tate, shifting from one foot to the other and chewing on
his lip. He was acting more skittish than a newborn colt.

"Sheriff, could I have a few words with you."

Tate gestured toward one of the mahogany chairs.
"Why don't you take a seat. You look like you could
use it."

"I'd prefer to stand, sir."

Tate almost choked. "Please stop calling me sir. It
makes me feel ancient. Last time I checked we're about
the same age. Not to mention you're one of my closest friends."

"Sorry, Tate, er, Sheriff. It's just that I always called
Sheriff Keegan, sir."

Tate swung his cowboy boots onto the desk and
placed his hands behind his head. "Relax, Cullen. I'm
sheriff of West Falls, but I'm not Joe Keegan. While I

always want to command respect, I don't want to instill fear."

Joe Keegan had been sheriff of West Falls as far back as Tate could remember. He'd ruled the town with an iron fist that had most of the deputies in the department quaking in their boots. Although Keegan was respected, he hadn't been very well liked. Tate had no desire to follow in his intractable footsteps.

"While you were out of the office we've fielded a few calls about…Cassidy Blake."

Tate bristled at the mention of her name.

"Cassidy? What kind of calls have been coming in about her?" he asked, his throat as dry as sandpaper. A niggling suspicion began to grow inside him. *No, it couldn't be.* Surely the people of West Falls had more sense than to dig up old skeletons.

"It seems word has gotten around that she's back in town. Some folks aren't too happy about it. They're saying she was never brought up on charges for the accident that injured Holly."

Tate slammed his fist on the desk, heat burning his cheeks as Cullen's words sunk in.

"No charges were ever brought because it was an accident," he protested. "She was all of eighteen years old, with a new driver's license in her pocket." He spoke through gritted teeth. "Holly decided not to press charges because she knew it was an accident…a tragic freak accident."

A tragic freak accident. It was amazing how passionately he could defend Cassidy when he himself had never stopped blaming her for Holly's condition.

As if her ears had been burning, his sister barreled into his office without so much as a knock to announce her arrival. Once inside she swiveled her chair around and pushed the door closed with a loud bang. He watched her glance up at Cullen, then cast him a smile before she glanced over at Tate. With a look of grim determination she maneuvered her wheelchair right next to his desk. She met her brother's gaze with wild frantic eyes. With a sinking sensation in his chest, Tate realized that the town gossips must have been working overtime.

Lord, please give me the strength to support my sister as she grapples with this news.

"Is it true what they're saying, Tate?" Holly asked. "Has Cassidy really come back to town?"

Chapter Three

Tate hated the despair he saw in Holly's eyes. Although he knew Cassidy had every right to come back and care for her mother, another part of him wanted to run her out of town. His sister was the type of person who'd worn her heart on her sleeve ever since she was a little girl. At the moment there was such a look of longing in her eyes. It was almost too much for him to bear.

"Tell me! Is it true?" she asked, her upper body tense as she tilted forward in her wheelchair.

"Yeah, it's true," he admitted. "She's back in town."

Her eyes grew wider at his terse acknowledgement. "How do you know?"

He let out a sigh. "I saw her with my own eyes."

She sat back and let out a few deep breaths. Cullen moved closer to her, his eyes full of concern, his arm draped around her shoulder as he asked, "Are you okay? Do you need some water?"

"I'm fine. I just didn't expect…after all this time, I wasn't sure she would ever come back." Her gaze shifted again to Tate. "What was it like, seeing her again? Did you talk to her?"

"Yes, we talked. She told me she's back for a while to visit with her family." He made no mention of Maylene Blake's health crisis or the car ride they'd shared over to her folks' house. Cassidy had asked him not to discuss her mother's medical condition, and he had no intention of breaking his promise.

"Did she… Did she mention me?" Holly looked down at her hands and began twirling her fingers round and round. She looked up at him expectantly, waiting for his response.

Tate looked at Holly, noting her flushed cheeks and her tight features. His concern was growing by the second over her state of mind. She'd dealt with so much over the past few years, both mentally and physically. Her spine hadn't been the only thing shattered. Her spirit had been broken, as well. Now news of Cassidy's return had struck her out of the blue, giving her the shock of her life. Yet, despite everything, she was still hoping Cassidy cared about her, still praying that she was in her thoughts and prayers.

It didn't take a rocket scientist to figure out that Holly was about to get emotionally crushed by the same woman who'd turned her world upside down years ago.

"No, she didn't mention you," he lied, hating himself for his deception as soon as the words rolled off his tongue. *Lord, please forgive me my trespasses.*

He watched Holly's face crumple, saw the tears gather in her cornflower-blue eyes and the way her slight shoulders slumped over. She muttered a few unintelligible words, then straightened herself up. She wheeled her chair around and fiddled with the door until it opened up, then sailed through it and down the hall until she was no longer visible.

Cullen raced out after her, his voice full of concern as he called out to her. "Holly! Wait. Please, don't go."

Although a part of him wanted to follow behind Cullen and tell Holly the truth, another part of him felt rooted to the spot. For the life of him, he couldn't move.

Lord, what is wrong with me? Why did I lie to Holly? Why couldn't I just tell her the truth?

Why? The answer was simple—because he couldn't bear the thought of his sister being hurt by Cassidy all over again. More than anyone he knew the heartache and pain Cassidy Blake could dole out. He'd been a victim of it, just as Holly had. Last time the betrayal had taken him by surprise, and the shock of it had brought him to his knees. This time, he vowed, he wasn't about to give Cassidy the chance to hurt him or Holly ever again.

"I still can't believe my baby girl is a famous artist. At least five of my friends have already called wanting you to autograph their paintings." Maylene added two sugars to her green tea and swirled the contents around in her cup. "I'm awfully proud of you, Cass."

Cassidy laughed at her mother's praise as she wrapped her fingers around her own steaming cup of tea. "Mom, I have a large, dedicated following in Phoenix, but I'm not famous."

Her mother reached out and tweaked her nose. "But you will be. With your talent, it's only a matter of time."

Cassidy grinned at her mother's crowing about her talent. Maylene had always been her biggest supporter, and even in the worst of times her devotion had never wavered. Being around her mother served as a shot of confidence that she sorely needed at the moment.

"The church bazaar is today," her mother said, her voice oozing excitement. "I was hoping you would come with us. It'll be one of my last outings before the surgery."

The Main Street Church bazaar was an annual fundraising event held out at the town fairgrounds. It had always been Cassidy's favorite church function. It was popular and drew the entire community. Cassidy felt panic rise up in her at the thought of being on public display. Although she wanted to face her past head-on, she had only been in town for two days. As far as she was concerned, it was too soon to attend the town's biggest social event. Facing Tate had nearly done her in. She couldn't imagine facing the entire town of West Falls all at once.

"Me? No, I can't go. I couldn't," she blurted out. Just the thought of running into her former classmates, schoolteachers and family friends made her skin itch.

Her mother's smile faded a bit and the twinkle in her eyes seemed to dim before Cassidy's eyes.

"I understand, honey," her mother said as she reached across the table and clasped her hand. "You're not ready to face everyone. Truthfully, I'm just so grateful you've come back home."

"Well, I don't understand, Maylene." Her father walked into the kitchen, clearly having heard the tail end of their conversation. "Cassidy has come back to help you, hasn't she? Won't it help you to have her attend the bazaar?"

"Harlan, it's fine," Maylene scolded, casting her husband a reproachful look that Cassidy had seen a hundred times or more throughout her childhood.

His mouth was set in a tight line, his jaw tightly clenched as he stood at the kitchen counter packing a picnic basket with sandwiches, chips, sodas and an assortment of fruits.

Big shock, Cassidy thought. Once again she'd earned her father's disapproval. It seemed there was nothing she could do to please him. On the other hand, all it took to please her mother was a simple act of courage.

Cassidy jumped up from her chair and placed her arms around her mother, squeezing her tightly as she said, "Daddy's right, Mama. I'm going to the bazaar."

Maylene clapped her hands together. "Are you sure? I don't want you to go if you're not ready."

She shrugged. "I'll probably never be completely ready. But, I'm a big girl. I can't hide out here forever."

Like it or not, she would soon be facing her deepest, darkest fear.

Lord, please stand by my side as I come face-to-face with my past.

Cassidy wondered if God might be sick and tired of listening to her prayers. After all, there were starving children all over the world and soldiers who stood in harm's way. Did God have time to worry about her past indiscretions? Did He still care about her?

God loves you. Cassidy repeated the affirmation in her head, drawing strength from the knowledge that God did indeed love her. That knowledge had been her one constant over the past few years. Through every step of her journey, she'd always known God was by her side. She knew not every prayer was answered, but He was still there listening.

Eight years ago she'd fled town with her tail between her legs. Those days were over. She was no longer a frightened eighteen-year-old lacking courage and faith. She was a grown woman who'd matured in her faith and who wanted to make amends for the past. But in doing so she would have to face the people she'd hurt the most.

Tate. The very thought of him caused goosebumps to pop up on her arms. There was so much she wanted to tell him, so many words she'd stored up inside her over the past eight years. Judging by the way he'd hightailed it away from her parents' house, Tate would sooner wrangle a rattlesnake than spend time alone with her again. But she wasn't going to give up. She would go down fighting if it meant she could bridge the distance between them. Even if he continued to resent her until the day he died, she was going to try her best to make amends.

It's never too late. The mantra played over and over in her mind, bolstering her confidence and providing her with inspiration. Her pastor in Phoenix had given her those encouraging words when she'd shared her past with him and confided her desire to make amends. It was the first time since the accident she'd dared to dream of forgiveness. And she still dreamed of it, even though she wasn't certain she deserved it.

Cassidy couldn't ignore the stares in her direction. They were too blatant and intrusive. Glares. Whispers. *Pastor's daughter.* Head shaking. Angry words being uttered just loud enough so she could hear them. Heat rose to her face as she heard the word *brazen* accompanied by a nasty glare in her direction. People who lived in small towns like West Falls never forgot scandals.

As much as she wanted to believe that she was a stronger person than the one who'd fled this town, all she wanted to do at the moment was run away. The only thing stopping her was her promise to Mama—and the small smidgen of pride she had left. She blinked back the tears and took a deep breath.

When she looked up Tate was standing there towering over her, his blue eyes filled with concern. She had to blink several times to make sure she wasn't imagining things. Nope, she wasn't hallucinating. He was still standing there with a questioning look on his face, his brows furrowed together.

The man was seriously good looking. More good looking than a man had a right to be. No man had ever looked better in a cowboy hat and jeans, she reckoned.

Tate Lynch had always been handsome. It had been the main reason she'd nurtured a mad crush on him all through middle school and junior high. That, and the kindness that flowed through him like water. Although he'd treated her with deference due to her status as his little sister's best friend, Cassidy had longed to see a glimmer of interest in his eyes. And then a funny thing had happened the summer before her sophomore year in high school. She'd grown four inches, the baby fat had turned to womanly curves and her acne had cleared up, leaving her with a flawless complexion. Tate had taken notice of the new and improved Cassidy and asked her out. They had dated all through high school, becoming engaged soon after she'd graduated.

"Cassidy, are you all right?" Tate asked, the tenderness in his voice warming her insides.

"I'm fine," she answered with a shaky smile, a bit unnerved about Tate's close proximity. His nearness made her wish for things she knew she could never have.

He scowled, his eyes raking over her face. "You don't look fine." He glanced around and made eye contact with a few of the townsfolk who had been eyeballing her. A fierce look was etched on his face as he drew himself up to his full height and crossed his arms across his chest. He seemed poised for battle. Most of them scampered away as soon as Tate glared in their direction. With a satisfied expression, he swung back around to face Cassidy.

"Were they bothering you?" Tate's eyebrows were furrowed and his mouth was set in a grim line. Turbulent emotions swirled in his eyes.

"I think they were just trying to make me feel unwelcome," she said with a shaky laugh. "Mission accomplished."

His expression darkened. "They don't have the right to persecute you. Or heckle you," he growled. "That's crossing the line."

Cassidy glanced around at the crowd of people milling around the fairgrounds. "It doesn't surprise me. West Falls is a small town. They still haven't forgiven me. And I can't say I blame them. Pastors' daughters aren't expected to fall from grace."

Tate raised an eyebrow. He kept quiet, seemingly waiting for her to explain herself.

"What I did was wrong. The accident…at least I can

say it was an accident. But running off, leaving West Falls like that, it was a horrible thing to do."

Surprise flashed in Tate's eyes, and for a moment he seemed speechless.

He blinked. "So you regret leaving?"

"Of course I do. I don't think you can solve your problems by running away from them." *Especially when you carried around in your heart everything you'd left behind.*

Tate flinched, his features hardening at her words. Something shifted between them in that moment, leaving the air between them highly charged. She had no idea what she'd done to cause a change in his demeanor, but she could sense he'd put up a wall between them.

"Are you here with your family?" he asked in a brisk voice.

"Yes, my parents are over by the wishing tree."

She felt a burst of pride at the thought of the wishing tree. At the age of seven she had come up with the idea of creating a wish list of needed items for her father's church that the congregation could individually select and donate. The items were then displayed on a wishing tree for everyone to see during the bazaar.

"Why don't I walk you over there in case there's any trouble."

This was the Tate she remembered. Ever the gentleman. Always ready to step in and help out those in need.

"You don't have to be my bodyguard, Tate. I'll be fine," she protested, struggling to hide her deflated spirits.

She didn't want Tate to feel obligated to escort her through the fairgrounds. After all they'd meant to each other, the last thing she wanted him to feel toward her was duty. He'd made it crystal clear yesterday that he wanted nothing to do with her. She knew he was probably feeling torn between his duty as sheriff and his disdain for her.

"It's my job to make sure every citizen in town is safe. That includes you," he said gruffly.

"Whatever you say, Sheriff," she said, placing emphasis on his title. She knew better than to argue with a stubborn Tate. Now that he was sheriff, she would wager he was even more strong-willed than ever.

As they walked side by side she couldn't help but notice the curious stares and doubletakes. She wasn't sure whether it was solely due to her presence or the fact that they were walking together. Everyone in town knew their dating history as well as their stormy breakup. Tate didn't seem to notice. Either that, she realized, or he was playing it cool. Occasionally he would tip his hat to someone or shout out a friendly greeting. At all times he carried himself with dignity and authority. He had a rugged kind of swagger that commanded attention.

Cassidy had so many wonderful memories of the bazaar—eating cotton candy, entering the greased pig contest, winning the whipped-cream-eating competition. She had always enjoyed the camaraderie of the congregation and the opportunity to spend the day with her friends. And Tate. Memories of the two of them riding the Ferris wheel, walking hand in hand and playing skeet ball rose unbidden to her mind.

"Oh my! Is that you, Cassidy Blake?"

A tall, regal-looking woman stood in her path, her hands planted firmly on her hips. Before she could say a word Cassidy found herself enveloped in a bear hug. The heavy scent of lilacs rose to her nostrils, bringing with it strong memories of childhood. Mona Jackson was one of her mother's oldest and most faithful friends. With her larger-than-life personality, Mona had always been one of Cassidy's favorite residents of West Falls. Now more than ever she was thrilled to see a friendly face.

"Mrs. Jackson. It's great to see you," Cassidy said, granting Mona her most genuine smile of the day.

Mona wagged a finger at her. "Don't you dare call me Mrs. Jackson. You're grown enough now to call me Mona."

Cassidy nodded. "Okay. Mona it is."

"I just talked to your Mama last night. I've never heard her so chipper and upbeat. That's because of you, Cassidy." Mona gave her a knowing look. "You're the best medicine there is. And before you leave town again I want you to autograph one of your paintings for me."

"Why don't you come by the house," she suggested, "and I'll personalize it for you."

"I'll make sure to do that. Good afternoon, Sheriff," Mona said with a nod at Tate.

Tate tipped his cowboy hat in Mona's direction. "Nice to see you, Mona."

Mona turned toward Tate, her eyes dancing with mischief as she said, "Have you ever seen a more beautiful woman in your life than this one?"

He tucked his hands into his front pockets and shifted from one foot to the other. "Er… No, I haven't. Cassidy has always been drop dead gorgeous." He turned his head to look at her. "And she still is."

Mona nodded her head in agreement. "Good to see you still have some sense. I'll catch y'all later. I'm off to buy some raffle tickets."

As soon as Mona walked off, Cassidy began talking a mile a minute. "I'm sorry she put you on the spot. That was so awkward. I mean…she practically forced you to agree with her—"

Tate rolled his eyes. "You act as if she twisted my arm. You are, and always will be, the most beautiful woman I've ever known."

Cassidy felt heat rising to her cheeks. She was awestruck by Tate's words. "You're sweet," she murmured, too overwhelmed to say anything more meaningful.

"Not sweet. Just truthful."

They continued walking until she came to an abrupt stop in front of one of the concession stands. Tate stopped in his tracks and shot Cassidy a look of confusion.

She pointed to the concession stand. "Do you mind if I stop and get some cotton candy?"

A smile tugged at the corners of his mouth. "You still love the pink sticky stuff, huh?"

Cassidy rubbed her stomach and licked her lips. "You have no idea," she answered. "Visions of cotton candy have been dancing around in my head all day."

"Knock yourself out," Tate said as he stepped into the line alongside her.

As soon as the confection was placed in her hand, she began to attack it with gusto. She held it out and offered it to Tate, who crinkled up his face in response. Cassidy shrugged, then kept on eating the sweat treat, finishing it in a matter of minutes.

He led her through the livestock enclosure as a short-cut toward getting back to the wishing tree. Cassidy paused for a moment to admire a brood of piglets sucking noisily at their mama's teats.

"You've got some cotton candy on your face," Tate said with a grin. "You always did end up wearing more of it than you ate."

His words resurrected old memories of their high school days, as well as all the church bazaars and carnivals they'd attended together. For Cassidy it almost felt as if they'd stepped back in time to the familiar rhythms of adolescence.

This is the way we were, she thought, *before the bottom fell out of our world.*

Tate reached out and wiped the cotton candy off her chin and lips, his fingers lingering a bit longer than necessary. She looked up at him, marveling at the way he made her feel. She couldn't remember the last time she'd felt so lighthearted, so joyful. And judging by the way he was looking at her, his eyes twinkling with glee, he felt the same way. For the moment it seemed as if all his anger toward her had faded away.

"And you were always there to wipe it off my face," she countered. "Or kiss it off."

As soon as the words rolled off her tongue, she wanted to yank them back in. She'd gotten carried away by their carefree banter and fallen into the familiar rhythms they'd once shared as a couple. Eight years ago it would've been nothing to make a comment like that. But now? After everything that had happened, it seemed flippant and overly familiar.

Tate's guarded expression said it all. *She'd gone too far.*

The air suddenly felt charged with electricity as Tate fidgeted with his collar and shifted his gaze to the ground. "That was a long time ago. A lifetime ago."

Her cheeks felt flushed, and she raised her palms to her face. "I know it was. I'm so sorry I brought that up. The bazaar, the cotton candy, being back home... it's bringing back a lot of memories," she explained as embarrassment flowed through her at her forward comment.

He brushed his hand across his face and let out a sigh. "It's not your fault. I got caught up in the past, too. Being with you reminds me of how things used to be. But those are just memories. Here and now, you and I are strangers." His face hardened, his mouth tightened. There was a hard edge to his voice. "You made sure of that when you ran away and never looked back." He let out a harsh laugh. "That's the way you wanted it, wasn't it? I think you called it closure."

His words were like daggers to her heart. *Strangers*? They'd grown up together, loved each other, had planned to spend the rest of their lives together. Did he truly believe she'd wanted the two of them to be strangers? Had she really used the word *closure* when she'd ended their engagement? It sounded so cold, so unfeeling under the circumstances.

"I've got to get out of here," he huffed. "I can't do this right now." His face resembled a storm cloud about to burst as he strode past her.

"Wait. Tate, please don't go. I need to talk to you," she pleaded.

There are so many things I never got to say. So many apologies I have yet to put into words.

He shook his head. "There's really nothing more to talk about. I respect the reasons why you came back, but it's got nothing to do with me."

"We have everything to talk about. The accident, why I left town, Holly."

He sliced his hand through the air. "That's all in the past. I've moved on."

Moved on? She was pretty sure Tate hadn't moved on. His anger toward her showed that he still had a lot of stuff he was holding on to. Not that she could blame him. He'd been in the middle of the firestorm and gotten burned at both ends. He had every right to resent her, but he needed to own it rather than pretend it was all in the past, dead and buried.

"I guess I haven't moved on, not completely," she admitted. "I know I can't change the past, but I can try and make amends for what I did. To Holly. And your family. And you."

Tate clenched his fists. "Nothing can be served by dredging all this up. If you need to make amends, do that with God, Cassidy. It's a little too late to come looking for forgiveness."

Too late for forgiveness? How could that be? Although she struggled with the notion that she was worthy of forgiveness, she knew it was possible. Every time she read the Bible she sought out scriptures to support the idea of being forgiven. No Bible passage said it more eloquently than Matthew 6:12. *Forgive us our debts as we forgive our debtors.*

Tate's words shocked her to the core. She'd expected

anger from him, but she hadn't anticipated him drawing a line in the sand, one he'd never allow her to cross
over. She could only imagine his fury if the truth about
the accident ever came to light.

"You've always been a man of faith," she said in a
bewildered voice. "If that's true, how can you be so
unforgiving?"

For a moment he didn't answer her. He stood there
like a statue, his eyes shooting daggers at her. His
breathing sounded choppy and ragged. His eyes resembled glaciers—cold and unapproachable. His hands
were clenched at his sides.

"I may be a man of faith, but even faith has limits.
As long as my sister is still sitting in a wheelchair, I'm
going to find it a bit difficult to forgive the woman who
put her there."

Chapter Four

Tate briskly walked away from the enclosure, nearly barreling headfirst into a pair of lovesick teenagers who crossed his path.

"Watch where you're going!" he yelled as he stared down the couple, who were holding hands and making goo-goo eyes at each other. One word from him had them letting go of each other's hands and muttering profuse apologies. For a moment he just stared at them as he battled the temptation to warn them about the perils of young love.

What good would it do? he asked himself. His teenaged self would never have listened to any adult advising him against falling in love with Cassidy. It had felt way too good at the time. And he'd been convinced that their love would last a lifetime. *Young, stupid love*.

At least he'd never been foolish enough to repeat that particular mistake again. Ever since then his heart had been off-limits.

He should never have sought out Cassidy at the bazaar. From the moment he'd arrived at the fairgrounds his radar had been on high alert. His gut instinct had told him that some of the townsfolk wouldn't be able to resist hassling her. At first he'd watched from the sidelines before allowing himself to step into the breach. He hadn't been able to stop himself. The sight of a vulnerable Cassidy, fighting back tears, had torn him up inside. Even when they were kids he'd never been able to resist playing the role of her protector. Clearly, not a lot had changed in that regard.

The moment he'd clapped eyes on her decked out in a romantic floral dress and a pair of tomato-red cowboy boots his heart had nearly popped out of his chest. It had been near impossible to keep his eyes off her.

It's not like she's the only beautiful woman in town, he reasoned with himself. But it wasn't just about beauty, was it? It was about heart and soul and a hundred other things he couldn't define.

The tender feelings she evoked in him left him feeling frustrated and unsure of himself. He could've sworn those feelings were dead and buried. He'd fallen out of love with Cassidy years ago. But this afternoon when he'd been in her presence, he'd felt more joyous than he'd felt in years. He'd felt alive. Wonderfully, achingly alive. And he hated himself for being so weak-minded, so up and down with his emotions.

But wasn't it only natural to remember all they'd shared? Love. Friendship. Joy. Dreams of forever. It was so easy to slip back into the familiar rhythms of the past, to relive the glory days of their love story. He imagined it was normal to replay the past and how things used to be. But what he was feeling seemed so much bigger, so much more powerful than just a walk down memory lane. It seemed real.

Don't be an idiot! There were so many things that trumped the old feelings she was bringing back. Holly. Loyalty. Betrayal. Honor.

Cassidy's own words had caused him to second-guess everything he was feeling.

I don't think you can solve your problems by running away from them.

When those words had come flying out of her mouth he'd almost challenged her on the spot. But his pride had reined him in. Had he been one of the problems she'd been running from? Is that why she'd called off their wedding and run off to another life in Phoenix?

It was all so confusing to him. The past he'd worked so hard to make peace with had caught up with him. How was he supposed to feel with Cassidy back in town and reminding him of everything he'd lost? He shut his eyes and did the one thing he knew would soothe his soul. Prayer. The only good thing that had come out of the accident was his relationship to God. In the ensuing days, weeks and months he'd turned to God to see him through Cassidy's desertion and Holly's paralysis. It had been the only solid thing he'd been able to hold on to when everything else in his life was falling apart.

And through prayer he'd learned the most important lesson of all. That the greatest peace lay in placing your burdens before God. *Lord, please help me to deal with all my bitterness toward Cassidy. Help me to truly walk the path toward forgiveness and not harbor any anger or resentment.*

"What's got you looking so twisted up?"

The sound of Holly's voice interrupted his prayers. He turned to his sister, noting the smirk on her face and the twinkle in her eye. She was wearing a T-shirt with the words This is How I Roll emblazoned on it, along with a picture of a wheelchair. Against his will Tate felt the corners of his mouth turning upward in a smile. As usual Holly's indomitable spirit was awe-inspiring.

"What makes you think I'm twisted up about something?"

Holly smirked. "For starters you look madder than Rooster Cogburn."

Rooster Cogburn was the Lynch family rooster. He was legendary for his feisty temperament. He ruled the Lynches' ranch with an iron fist and raised a ruckus every morning at the crack of dawn. They'd named him after one of their favorite John Wayne movies.

"Not to mention the fact that you're walking around mumbling under your breath," she added with a knowing look. "That's always a clear giveaway that you're aggravated."

Tate nodded, acknowledging Holly's assessment. "I am…a little annoyed. But it's no big deal. It'll all blow over."

Blow over? Yeah, right! It hadn't blown over in eight years.

"Humph. If you say so." Holly was eying him skeptically, as if she didn't believe him for a second.

He raised an eyebrow and scowled at his sister. "It isn't every day I get compared to the family rooster."

Holly threw her head back and laughed. "Take it as a compliment. Rooster Cogburn has more personality than anyone I've ever known."

Tate chuckled. Holly always had a knack for making him laugh.

"I need to tell you something." His voice turned serious.

"I'm listening. Go ahead."

Tate steeled himself. If there was one thing Holly valued more than anything it was honesty. He hadn't done the right thing yesterday and it had been eating him up inside all day.

"I didn't tell you the truth," he admitted, his eyes flicking from his sister's face down to the ground. "Cassidy did ask about you. She wanted to know how you were doing."

Holly's mouth swung open. Her eyes narrowed and she shot him a look of disgust.

"Why did you lie to me?"

"I didn't want you being pulled in by her and getting hurt again."

"That's not your choice to make!" she exploded. "The last time I checked I'm a grown woman."

He nodded curtly. "I know, but old habits die hard. I've spent most of my life watching out for you. If I saw a Mack truck speeding toward you, I'd pull you out of the way, wouldn't I?"

Holly threw her hands in the air. "It's not about me anymore. It's about you. You and your relationship with Cassidy."

He bristled. "There's nothing between me and Cassidy. That ended a long time ago."

Holly arched an eyebrow. "But you never really closed the door on it." She cocked her head to the side. "All these years and you've barely looked at another woman."

Tate snorted. What was Holly talking about? He'd

dated Kit Saunders, a local attorney, for almost two years. Since their breakup two years ago he'd been fixed up on dozens of blind dates by his friends.

"Kit and I were in a long-term relationship."

Holly rolled her eyes. "Seemed more like convenience than romance."

"I'll have you know I've been on plenty of dates since then!" he protested.

"How many of 'em were second dates?"

Second dates? He hadn't even thought of second dates. Until now. *Why haven't I had any second dates?* "I'm town Sheriff. I live a busy lifestyle, and my work comes first. When the time is right I'll fall in love, settle down and have a few babies you can sing lullabies to at night. I'm more than ready to move on."

Holly looked at him, a somber expression etched on her face. "I don't think you'll be able to move on until you forgive Cassidy."

"It's not easy to forgive someone who—"

"Who what? Broke your heart? Called off your wedding? Put me in this chair?"

Tate shot Holly a fierce look. "You know it's way more complicated than that. When I look at you in that wheelchair—"

Tears glistened in Holly's eyes. She furiously blinked them away. "Don't you dare hide behind me, Tate. If you want to hate her for the rest of your life, then do it. But don't you dare pretend that it's all for my benefit." She huffed noisily. "Because we both know that's the biggest lie of all."

Without a word of goodbye, Holly turned from him and wheeled away.

First Doc. Now Holly. Both of them had given him a reality check. He couldn't ignore the truth when it was staring him straight in the face. His bitterness wasn't about the accident. It was about the way she'd treated him—the way she'd left him high and dry, dreaming of a future that would never come to pass. It was about his embarrassment, his shame, his feeling like a prize fool in front of the entire town. It was about losing someone that once meant the world to him. It was about loss.

Tate raked his hands through his hair and let out a deep shudder. Love. It was such a simple word for such a complicated emotion. When he'd fallen in love with the pastor's daughter, it had all seemed so uncomplicated. Effortless. It had felt like such a blessing to meet his soul mate at such a young age. Their future had looked so promising. But in one fell swoop everything had been taken away from him. And every time he thought about it, he burned up inside.

Truth to be told, he missed being in love. He ached to feel that rush again, to feel so at one with another person that he didn't know where he began and she ended. He missed imagining what their kids would look like and dreaming of growing old together. He missed belonging to someone.

Not just someone, he realized with a sinking feeling in his gut. Try as he might to deny it, he missed belonging to Cassidy.

The crowd cheered and shouted words of encouragement as the eight contestants in the pie eating contest vied neck and neck for the win. The contest came to a riveting conclusion as a cherub-faced girl, who couldn't have been more than eighty pounds soaking wet, raised her hands in the air as the victor. Grown men three times her size clutched their stomachs, their faces showing queasiness. Cassidy and her mother laughed at the sight of all the contestants' faces covered in blue-berries and cream. Cassidy pulled out her camera and snapped a few pictures of the participants, wanting to capture the lighthearted moment on film.

"If I haven't already told you, it means the world to us that you joined us today. I can't think of the last time I've had so much fun," her mother said, her face beaming with joy.

"You've said it a dozen times or more," Cassidy an-swered with a chuckle. "But it never gets old hearing it. And if I haven't already told you, I'm happy to be back."

Her mother fanned herself with her hand. "If only it weren't so hot today. This feels like August weather, not May."

"Mom, are you sure you're not thirsty? I could get you some iced tea or a bottled water at the conces-sion stand." She narrowed her eyes as she looked at her mother. Tiny beads of sweat were gathered on her forehead and her face looked washed-out.

Her mother waved her off. "No thanks, sweetheart. I'm feeling a little nauseous at the moment. I'm not sure if I could keep it down."

The fact that her mother was experiencing nausea concerned her. Perhaps it was time they left the bazaar and headed home. Although it had been a fun day, it had also been a taxing one for her mother due to the hot weather and the extensive amount of walking she'd done around the fairgrounds. Cassidy glanced around the crowded area looking for her father, anxious to let him know her mother was feeling poorly.

"Why don't we go sit down in the shade so you can rest a bit," she suggested, reaching out to grasp her by the elbow. Her mother swayed a bit to one side, her body sagging as she crumpled to the ground.

"Mama!" Cassidy cried out, falling to her knees next to her mother in the dirt. Her mother was lying on her back, her head lolled to one side. The contents of her purse had scattered around her. A group of people crowded around, looking on and speaking in hushed tones. She reached for her mother's wrist so she could take her pulse. Her concern grew when it registered as thready and weak. Panic seized hold of her as the gravity of the situation settled in.

"Somebody, please call an ambulance," she cried out as fear gripped her by the throat.

A young woman bent down and began collecting the items that had fallen from her mother's purse. Cassidy was gazing out into the crowd, praying that her father would return to the area. She saw Tate, with his broad shoulders and commanding air, surging forward through the crowd. He moved quickly toward where she knelt on the ground next to her mother, his gaze full of concern as he searched her face for answers.

"Cass, what happened?" he asked as he lowered himself to the ground.

She bit her lip in an effort to hold back the tide of tears that threatened to overwhelm her. Seeing her mother lying on the ground in such a vulnerable state brought a host of emotions to the surface. What she was feeling most was fear. Fear of losing her mother.

Fear of not doing the right thing in this moment. Fear that she'd never get back the years she'd lost with her.

Her voice trembled as she explained, "We were standing here talking and she told me she felt nauseous. Then she fainted. I'm having a hard time rousing her."

Tate reached down and gently swatted Maylene's face, then loosened the silk scarf around her neck. A little bit of color seemed to be returning to her cheeks.

"Maylene!" The sound of her father's voice rang out in the crowd. She watched as her father stepped past the crowd and scrambled to his wife's side. He bent over beside her, reaching out and caressing the side of his wife's face. The loving embrace brought tears to Cassidy's eyes. It made her feel humble to witness the deep and abiding love of her parents. She found herself wishing for things she'd let go of a long time ago.

Her mother let out a low moan and her eyes fluttered open. For a moment she appeared disoriented. "Cassidy! What are you doing here?"

She reached out and patted her mother's hand. "I'm here for the summer, Mama. Don't you remember?" she asked, sniffing back tears, her heart pounding with fear.

"Of course I do, honey. I just feel so woozy. Everything is spinning."

"Don't try to get up, darling. Let's wait for the medics to arrive," her father advised.

The sound of an ambulance siren blared in the distance, sounding closer and closer by the second. Cassidy stood up and scanned the area, realizing that the paramedics wouldn't be able to maneuver the ambulance through the small space between the enclosure and the concession stands.

She turned to Tate, pointing in the direction of the ambulance. "They won't be able to get through here. It's too narrow," she fretted.

"Don't worry. I've got her," Tate said. "Just hold onto my neck, Maylene," he advised just before bending down and lifting her up in his arms, treating her as if she were as fragile as a newborn babe. As he instructed, she wrapped her hands around his neck and held on for dear life.

"Move back everyone," he instructed the crowd, who immediately fanned out to let him get by.

The ambulance pulled up outside the enclosure and two paramedics jumped out, quickly opening up the back of the ambulance when they saw Tate striding toward them with Maylene in his arms. Cassidy and her father were right at his heels.

"I'd like to ride with your mother," her father said to Cassidy, his eyes full of uncertainty. "Could you please drive my car over to the hospital?" he asked, handing her his key fob, his hand visibly trembling.

Cassidy reached for the keys and nodded to her father. Still feeling a bit dazed, she murmured, "I'll be there shortly."

Her father squeezed her hand and climbed into the back of the ambulance, taking a seat next to his wife. As the paramedics closed the door, she could see him touching her mother's face and placing a kiss on her cheek. The tender gesture cracked her heart wide open, making her feel more vulnerable than she'd allowed herself to feel in a very long time.

Cassidy stared at the retreating ambulance as it carried her mother away, tears streaming down her face, her shoulders heaving with emotion. Tate felt his insides being squeezed at the sight of her solitary figure, alone and hurting. He battled the impulse to wrap his arms around her, not knowing if it would be an intrusion.

Tate moved toward her, wanting to let her know she wasn't alone. He could see what it was doing to her. It made him ache inside to see her broken up like this. It made him feel guilty for having been so abrupt with her earlier.

"She's going to be just fine," he said, trying to make his words sound reassuring. "It's probably just heat stroke."

Lord, please don't make a liar out of me. Please don't let this be a setback for Maylene.

"You don't know that," she said, her voice breaking under the strain. Vibrant green eyes studied him and he could see it all in their depths—fear, uncertainty, panic.

"Tate, I'm scared. What if I've come back after all this time only to lose her? I'll never forgive myself." Her voice was tight with emotion.

"Don't think like that. Just pray, Cass. Tell God what's in your heart. Let him know how scared you are." It's what he'd done in the days and weeks after the accident—he'd put it all out there in the hopes that God was listening to his prayers. And He had been. Tate knew it with a certainty. That experience had forever changed him into a believer.

He pulled Cassidy to him, wrapping his arms around her and smoothing back her strawberry blond mane. She smelled of strawberries and vanilla, reminding him of lazy summer nights and stolen kisses in her mother's rose garden. He heard her muffled sobs, felt the heaving of her chest as she vented her fear and sorrow. Her arms grabbed him around the waist as if he were a lifeline. She clung to him for a few moments—brief moments when he wanted nothing more than to comfort her and give her a soft place to fall.

Just when he'd thought he was done with Cassidy, he felt himself being pulled back into her world.

After a few minutes she untangled herself from his arms. "I should get going to the hospital." She let out a ragged sigh. "I really need to find out what's going on with Mama. I'm sure Daddy is frantic with worry."

"Go, Cassidy. Be with your family." The thought of her being at the hospital supporting her family made him feel warm inside. He had a hunch that most of the congregation would check up on the family and make sure they were fed and cared for. It was one of the many strengths of Main Street Church—its members came together in times of trouble.

She flashed him a tight smile. "Thanks for everything. Really. You always know what to do in a crisis, Tate."

"Keep me posted, okay?" he called after her. "I'll be at the Sheriff's Office."

"Will do," she shouted as she hurried off. He watched her as she located her father's car in the lot and gained entry to the vehicle, the tires spewing dirt and dust as she took off.

For what seemed like an eternity he paced back and forth, his mind filled with thoughts of Cassidy and her parents. He knew it was dangerous to get caught up in Cassidy's life, but he couldn't help himself. Pastor Blake and Maylene had always treated him like a member of their family. He couldn't pretend he didn't care about their well-being. With a groan of surrender he made his way to his car and jumped in, revving the engine as if he was racing in the Indy 500. In record time he made it across town to Trinity Hospital.

A portly nurse directed him to the seventh floor when he arrived at the emergency room. After taking a short elevator ride he found Cassidy sitting on a sofa outside room 723, her hands clasped in prayer. When she glanced up and saw him standing there, relief washed over her face.

"Tate! What are you doing here?"

"I just wanted to check on your mother's condition. How is she?" He jammed his hands into his front pockets and rocked a bit on the heels of his cowboy boots.

"The doctors are still in with her. They let Daddy stay, but they won't let me inside." She raked a hand through her wayward curls. "It feels like I've been waiting out here for forever."

"Patience is a virtue," Tate quipped, the corners of his mouth twitching with amusement.

Cassidy smiled back at him, filling him with satisfaction that he'd been able to provide her with a little distraction.

"I used to hate when Daddy said that. It always seemed as if he was staring straight at me when he said it."

He smiled at the memory. Cassidy couldn't have been more than eight years old. He'd been a year and a half older, but only one year ahead of her in class. Kids within a certain age range were grouped together for

Bible Class so he'd been alongside Cassidy and Holly. Pastor Blake had been their teacher.

"I think he was trying to send you a message. From what I remember, you weren't the most patient of children." Tate sat down next to Cassidy and settled in.

Cassidy made a face. "As I said then, patience is for old people and fools." She giggled, spurred on by the memory of her eight-year-old self.

"I don't think I've ever seen your father more angry," Tate said, surrendering to a full-on chuckle. "Didn't he kick you out of class?"

"Yep," she answered with a grin. "I had to sit in his office and write the phrase patience is a virtue one hundred times. To this day I don't understand why it's such a virtue. Even as a kid I always ripped through my Christmas presents in record time."

"I suppose that was the downside of being the pastor's daughter. Having your father teach Bible Class couldn't have been much fun. You never got away with a single thing."

"Tell me about it," she said with a groan.

"Was it that bad?"

"Not always. There were lots of good things about being a pastor's daughter. But the expectations…I can't say I enjoyed that part. I held a lot inside." Her face held a wistful expression. "I wish I'd been allowed to fail as many times as I flew. It wouldn't have been so devastating when it all fell apart. Does that make sense?"

Tate nodded. "It makes perfect sense. Failing would have given you some perspective." His voice got quiet. "I wish you would've told me that back then. Maybe you wouldn't have felt so alone."

How could he not have seen all her turmoil? They'd been so close, practically joined at the hip. His thoughts were full of the past, full of his relationship with Cassidy. More than anything he'd thought they'd shared a solid friendship. Perhaps if he'd known all the pressure she'd been under, things might have been different. Perhaps she wouldn't have hightailed it out of town when everything had gone so terribly wrong. At least now he understood how much stress she'd been under leading up to the accident.

She wrinkled up her nose. "I don't think I was very honest with myself back then," she admitted. "I was too busy keeping up appearances. It took me several years to come to terms with things."

The hospital room door swung open with a creak, and Pastor Blake stepped out into the hallway. The strain of his wife's health crisis had left telltale signs on his face. Tight lines had formed at the sides of his mouth while his complexion had a grayish tinge. He'd never seen him look so vulnerable.

Cassidy jumped up from her seat, her eyes wide as she asked, "What are the doctors saying?"

Pastor Blake placed his hand on Cassidy's shoulder. "She's doing fine. They said she was dehydrated and hadn't taken in enough fluids or food today," Pastor Blake explained. "Basically, she overextended herself. Her immune system is weakened due to the chemo, so she really has to make sure to eat throughout the day and drink plenty of fluids. They're going to keep her in the hospital for a few days so they can stabilize her electrolytes and monitor her."

Cassidy's shoulders sagged with relief and she let out an emotional cry. "Thank the Lord!"

Tate reached out and clasped Pastor Blake's hand in a gesture of solidarity. Just then a few parishioners made their way toward them from the waiting room. Mona Jackson, Doc Sampson and Tate's deputy Cullen Brand were among them. As he watched Cassidy and her father draw comfort from the congregation, a feeling of peace settled around his heart. Cassidy was home, back in the bosom of her family and the congregation. Even though some people in West Falls objected to her being back in town, there were many others who rejoiced at her homecoming. It was what he loved most about his hometown—the way the community gathered together in times of hardship.

It was time for him to go. Now that he knew Maylene was fine and that the Blakes were being supported and loved, he had no business being here. It was way too dangerous to his peace of mind to be around her. He met Cassidy's gaze, letting her know with a hand motion that he was on his way out. She mouthed her thanks, then flashed him a sweet smile.

He felt Cassidy's eyes on him as he strode down the hallway. Although he was tempted to turn around and catch one last glimpse of her, he suspected it would only make the conflict raging inside him that much worse.

Chapter Five

The past forty-eight hours had been an emotional roller coaster. Although she was thankful her mother was being released from the hospital this afternoon, she was still consumed with worry about her health. She had spent the better part of the morning with her mother, meeting with her oncologist and discussing postsurgical options. Seeing her mother looking so fragile in her hospital bed had frightened her. It reminded her that life was a tenuous thing, impermanent and unpredictable.

At the moment her mother was downstairs in the oncology wing having some tests run. She was still scheduled for surgery in a few days, and the doctors were checking to see if her chemo treatments had reduced the size of her tumor. Even though Cassidy's main concern was her mother, a million questions about Tate were still rolling around in her head. Although it seemed at times that he was thawing toward her, there was still a gap between them the length of an ocean. Instead of working at making amends, she'd found herself daydreaming about what her life might have been like if she hadn't left town.

Would her life have been different if the accident had never happened? It was a question she liked to toss around in her head every now and again. Would she be married to Tate with a few children running her ragged? Or would they have outgrown each other and gone their separate ways?

If only she didn't have so many powerful memories of the two of them. She'd been happy then, hadn't she? And happy with the person she was whenever she was with him. With Tate, it had always been enough just to be herself. Which made it all the worse that she'd treated him so shabbily.

Had she made the worst mistake of her life in leaving West Falls?

Tears ran down her face, and her shoulders heaved under the weight of her sobs. Being home was so much more of an emotional journey than she'd anticipated. For someone who was used to hiding her feelings, it was therapeutic to allow herself to give in to the tidal wave. When her mother was wheeled back into the room, Cassidy didn't bother to conceal the fact that she'd been crying. She was done disguising her sentiments since all it had ever done was magnify them by tenfold.

"Baby, what's wrong?" Maylene asked as she stood up and hurried to her daughter's side. She sat down next to her on the hospital bed, placing her arms around Cassidy's shoulders and pulling her to her side, her eyes filled with compassion.

"I'm sorry, Mama," she said as she swiped at her eyes. "I don't know where all this is coming from. I'm supposed to be your rock, not the other way around."

She tried to collect herself. Right now her focus should be on her mother, not Tate.

"Shhhh. I'm your mother. That's my job," she cooed as she wiped away her tears. "To tell you the truth, I'm sick and tired of being poked and prodded. I need a distraction from all this talk about cancer. Talk to me. It's been so long since you've poured your heart out to me, Cass. I want to feel like your mother, not some invalid in a hospital bed."

Maylene was staring at her with pleading eyes. Perhaps she was scared and nervous about her upcoming procedure. Perhaps she was just tired of all the worrying about test results and surgery. Right now she just wanted to be Cassidy's mother. And Cassidy couldn't think of anything in the world that she needed more at this moment.

"I'm just so confused about Tate. I put my foot in my mouth the other day by asking about Holly. He gave me the big ole Texas slap down. Told me never to ask about Holly again." She sniffled to hold back the tears. "He said I don't deserve to ask about her. And he's right. What made me think I could ask about her?"

Her mother made tutting sounds. "No, he's not right. And he's not wrong either. He's a brother being protective of his sister. He always was, even before the accident. You know that. When you were kids he barely let her out of his sight. He's got a chip on his shoulder a mile wide, partly because of Holly's condition and partly because of the way you left. It really did break his heart."

Cassidy covered her face with her hands and let out

a shuddering sigh. The very thought of causing Tate so much pain rocked her to her core. And shamed her.

"Then my car broke down and he ended up giving me a ride home," she continued. "He was actually nice to me. But then he couldn't wait to leave. Same thing happened at the bazaar. We were talking and getting along fine until I made an off the cuff remark. He told me we were strangers. And then the other day he stopped by the hospital to check on us." She wrapped her arms around her middle. "I really want to make amends, but I keep hitting brick walls with him."

"He's a kind, generous man. It's in his nature to be that way, so I'm sure he's torn about how to treat you and how to feel about you. He's had a long time to let those wounds fester. He has a lot of pride. You can't expect him to pretend as if nothing ever happened." She reached out and grasped Cassidy by the chin, turning her face so that she could look her straight in the eye. "Please don't forget that God won't ever give you more than you can handle."

Her lips trembled with emotion. "Forgive me, Mama, but sometimes it seems as if He does give me more than I can handle. I wish I were strong like you."

"Cassidy Anne Blake! You are stronger than you know. I wish you could see that."

She drew a deep breath. "And it's not just Tate that's bothering me. Daddy can barely look me in the eye after all this time. I think he's ashamed that I'm his daughter."

Maylene made a tutting noise. "Your father loves you. He's never been ashamed of you a day in his life. I think he struggles with a lot of guilt since he's the one who suggested you leave town. He doesn't know if he

steered you on the right path, and that's hard for him."
She heaved a deep sigh. "That being said, he dealt with a
lot of fallout when you left. The Lynches wanted blood.
Your blood. Your father and I were the closest things
they could get to punishing you. I never told you the
whole of it. Perhaps I should have, but we didn't want
you to carry that burden. Led by Tate's parents, some
of the people in town circulated a petition to remove
your father as pastor."

"What? Daddy has led Main Street Church for almost twenty-five years. On what grounds were they
trying to oust him?"

Maylene crossed her hands in front of her. "They
believed he shouldn't be the spiritual leader of Main
Street Church under a morality clause."

"Morality?" Cassidy asked, her eyebrows coming
together in a frown. "That's ridiculous. He's the most
moral man in West Falls. He's never so much as—" Understanding came like a bolt out of the blue, and despite
the fact that she should have anticipated this twist, she
felt as if she'd been kicked in the stomach. Her throat
felt dry as sandpaper and it took her a moment to process her thoughts. "It was my morality they were questioning, wasn't it? Daddy was just the scapegoat."

Tears misted in her mother's eyes. "Yes, dear. Certain
people in town thought you got off scot-free." Maylene
scoffed. "As if you didn't suffer. They said it was im-
moral that you left town so soon after the crash. Some
were angry that no charges were filed against you."

"I'm so sorry." She sobbed. "If I'd known I would've
stayed and let them get their pound of flesh from me.
It's so unfair that they went after the two of you."

Maylene nodded, her expression full of understanding. "We made the decision as a family that you should leave West Falls. Emotions were too heated at the time. Sheriff Keegan was threatening to arrest you, there were rumors about the Lynches filing a civil suit, Regina and Jenna were being interrogated. It was a terrible time." Maylene shuddered at the recollection. "And regardless of what certain small-minded people tried to do, your father maintained his position with the full backing of the congregation, minus a few troublemakers."

Cassidy raised an eyebrow. "What about the Lynches? Are they still part of the congregation?"

Maylene sighed. "Here and there. Not regularly, although the whole family does turn out on holidays like Christmas and Easter. I'm happy to say that Holly and Tate are faithful worshipers though."

Holly. Her pulse quickened at the memory of her former best friend, the playmate she had been best buddies with since grade school. They had once been inseparable. Sisters of the heart. A sudden image of Holly flashed into her mind—her larger-than-life smile, the big blue eyes, her dirty blond hair that she could never get a comb through—and it served as a reminder of all she'd lost. She no longer had a best friend. There was no one in her life she could tell all her innermost secrets and fears.

"I'm glad she's part of the Church," she said in a wistful voice. "That means she has people to support her and to see her through all the ups and downs, the doctor's visits, the emotional turmoil."

Maylene pursed her lips. "Congregations are wonderful support systems, but nothing replaces a best friend.

I think you can be a help to her, now that you're back in town."

Hearing her mother's words caused frustration to bubble up inside her, then overflow. "How can I help her, Mama? I can't give her back the use of her legs," she snapped, struggling to keep her anger in check.

Her mother gazed at her, emerald eyes flashing with emotion. "Oh, Cassidy. Don't you see? Holly lost the use of her legs but she still has her faith, her family and her congregation. The one thing in her life she doesn't have is you."

Tate hadn't wanted to attend Sunday service this morning. Although he'd gotten closer to the Lord in the past few years and rarely missed a service, he'd almost bailed on church this morning. He had his reasons for not wanting to come today. And every single one of 'em was tied to Cassidy. Today would have been their eighth wedding anniversary, if Cassidy hadn't dumped him and skipped town. They would have exchanged vows in this very church. He swallowed past the lump in his throat, trying not to allow his mind to roam to the forbidden place.

If it wasn't for Holly's badgering him, he'd be at the ranch right about now checking on Fiddlesticks. His onyx Arabian mare was due to give birth soon, and he wanted to keep an eye on her. Although law enforcement was his calling, horses were his passion. He was devoted to them and spent every spare moment in their presence.

He had to admit it as he gazed at his surroundings. Main Street Church was a spectacular place to worship. With its stunning stained glass windows, Gothic architecture and burnished wooden pews it had a stately grandeur. There was no other place of worship like it. Sometimes he liked to sit for a spell in one of the pews when the church was empty. Just himself, the church and the big guy upstairs. It was during those times that he had his most deep conversations with the Lord.

As he followed Holly down the aisle he couldn't help but notice the furtive glances in their direction and the electricity crackling in the air. Pure instinct had him glancing toward the first pew at the front of the church. Air came rushing out of his lungs and he almost stopped midstride. Cassidy was sitting with Maylene and Regina in the Blake family pew. At the moment he and Holly were making their way to the pews at the left front of the church, directly opposite the Blakes.

It would be the first time Holly and Cassidy came face-to-face in eight long years. He let out a deep breath as Holly situated herself in the wheelchair accessible seating next to the pew. He clenched and unclenched his fists at his sides. Something had told him that Main Street Church wasn't a place he wanted to grace with his presence today. If only he had listened.

As Cassidy sat in the family pew listening to her father's sermon, she could feel the heat of prying eyes in her direction. Although the townsfolk were still grappling with her being back in town, she hadn't expected that reaction to extend to the church. Main Street Church was sacred. It had always been her safe place, her haven. And within its walls she'd always found acceptance. And love.

Could she really last a whole summer here? Would the whispers, comments and looks never end? She'd dealt with it the best she could at the church bazaar. Tate had made things a lot easier by stepping in and handling her hecklers. Nevertheless the animosity had still rattled her. It drove home the point that she no longer belonged. Not really.

Of course I'm going to stay. Mama needs me! And I need to be here to finally see things through. This time she wasn't running away. She was just going to have to develop a thicker skin. *What doesn't kill you makes you stronger.* Wasn't that the old adage? And she had to admit that the stares she was receiving today weren't filled with malice. They were more curious than nasty, she realized. Perhaps they were wondering about the return of the pastor's daughter and why she'd finally come home. She couldn't fault them for that.

She turned to her mother, letting her gaze roam over her graceful features. Cassidy envied her. She always seemed to be at such peace. Even as she struggled with a cancer diagnosis, her mother was steadfast in her faith and in her belief in God's healing. Today she was wearing an elegant scarf tied around her head rather than her auburn wig. It was close to eighty degrees outside, and her mother had complained about the wig being itchy on her scalp. Cassidy thought she looked lovely. Other than her fainting episode at the bazaar, no one would ever guess she was dealing with a deadly cancer.

The sudden buzz of whispers rippled through the church. What in the world was going on? She turned her head ever so slightly to the left, just enough so that she caught sight of Holly maneuvering herself down the aisle, followed by Tate. Goosebumps popped up on her arms. Tate met her gaze with a look of surprise and what appeared to be dismay. When Holly looked over, she felt her heart beating so fast she feared it would jump out of her chest. She braced herself for any sign of animosity in her expression. Instead Holly stared back at her, a hint of a smile on her lips. Shocked by the unexpected encounter, Cassidy turned away and stared front and center at the pulpit. She forced herself to try and concentrate on her father's sermon.

"The power of faith is a mighty thing." Her father's words rang out in the church, resonating with conviction and the rich timbre of his voice. "It can move mountains."

Cassidy felt her hand being squeezed by Regina, who was sitting on her right. She looked over at her cousin, buoyed by the encouraging smile and the support she was showing her. With a smile of her own, she squeezed her cousin's hand back.

After she managed to get her pulse beating at a normal pace she glanced over at the Lynches again, meeting Tate's gaze head on. He looked nervous. And worried. His brows were furrowed, and his handsome face was showing signs of tension. What was going on with him? Did the fact that she and Holly were in such close proximity bother him that much? What exactly did he think she was capable of doing?

Cassidy took out her hymnal and began singing along to one of her favorites, "Just a Closer Walk With Thee." As she sang along with the church choir and the congregation, strong memories came flooding back to her. As a child she'd been a member of the Main Street Church's children's choir, along with Regina, Holly and Jenna. It had been the genesis of their friendship. The church no longer had a children's choir, and she thought it was a pity. Children needed to know that they too had something to offer up to God. Listening to the purity and beauty of their little voices was a soul-stirring experience. It was truly a wondrous gift.

At the end of the service, Cassidy watched her father walk to the back of the church and greet the parishioners as they exited. As was her tradition, her mother joined her father in greeting the congregation. Holly sat across the way talking to Tate, her face animated as they exchanged words, going back and forth like a Ping Pong ball. Judging by Tate's stern expression, mingled with the mutinous look on Holly's face, she suspected that they were arguing. Most likely about her.

"What are you waiting for? Aren't you going to say hello?" Regina asked.

"I'm waiting for the butterflies to settle." Cassidy smoothed the fabric of her white cotton dress and fidgeted with the belt cinched around her waist.

"Don't wait too long," Regina warned. "Tate looks like he's about to hustle her out of here. Then again," she said as she glanced over at the Lynches, "I think Holly can hold her own. She looks mad enough to spit nails."

Cassidy glanced over Regina's shoulder, noticing the tension between the Lynches. Tate and Holly were incredibly close siblings and always had been. Causing friction in their relationship was the last thing she wanted to happen. But Tate needed to understand that she wasn't leaving Main Street Church without first having a heart-to-heart with Holly. Running away was no longer an option.

She threw her hands up in the air. "This is ridiculous! I'm just going to get this over with."

With a sigh of resignation she walked over to the Lynches, the jingling of her stacked bracelets heralding her arrival. Tate was facing her, his expression wary, arms folded across his chest. Their eyes met, and she could see the vulnerability in their icy blue depths. He wasn't angry, she realized. He was scared. Scared she was going to do something to hurt Holly again, she imagined.

I won't hurt her. She sent the message to him with her eyes, hoping he still believed in her enough to trust her. His face softened and he seemed a little more relaxed.

"Cassidy," Tate drawled, causing Holly to spin her chair around so that she was face to face with her.

Joy fluttered inside her—part of her felt as light and airy as a butterfly—as she looked at a face that was almost as familiar to her as her own.

Just then her father walked up. Holly's face lit up when she saw him. He greeted Tate with a smile and placed a comforting hand on his shoulder.

"Why don't you girls find a quiet place to talk," he suggested. "My office is empty. It will give you the privacy you need."

Holly and Cassidy looked at each other, both nodding in agreement. With a look of satisfaction on his face, her father ushered them toward the hallway. When Tate moved to follow them, he reached out and gently grabbed him by the arm.

"They don't need an audience, Tate. Whatever they have to say to each other should only be heard by one another. I know how you feel about protecting Holly, and frankly I feel the same way about Cassidy, but this is their moment."

Tate glanced over at his sister. "Is that okay with you?"

"You heard Pastor Blake," Holly admonished. "This is just between me and Cassidy."

Tate grimaced, then took a few steps back. Cassidy followed Holly down the hall to the church offices. When they reached his office her father opened up the door and ushered them inside. As Cassidy walked past him he winked at her and squeezed her arm.

"Take however long you need," he said before closing the door behind him.

As soon as the door closed Cassidy took a moment to look around her. Her father's office had always been her favorite place in Main Street Church. It was a cheery place, with sunlight streaming through the windows, a rich mahogany desk and chair as well as a comfy sofa and coffee table. In the corner sat a mini fridge that he stocked with Dr Pepper. She remembered many a day when she would curl up on the sofa when she was waiting around the church for her father.

"Cat got your tongue."

She turned to face Holly, getting her first up close and personal look at her for the first time in eight years. It was funny how a person could look the same, yet different. She was thinner, although her arms were way more muscular than they'd ever been in high school. She imagined the muscles were a result of using her arms to navigate her wheelchair. Her eyes were still cornflower blue, her hair still blond and a bit wild. She was still beautiful. Still Holly. And she still had that way of looking right through you and cutting straight to the chase.

Cassidy sucked in a deep breath. "I'm going to take a seat," she said, seating herself in one of the antique cherrywood chairs that had belonged to one of her great-greats. "I don't think these legs of mine are going to hold up."

Holly narrowed her eyes. "You're nervous."

"Yes, I am. Silly, isn't it. We were best friends for eleven years, and I can barely look you in the eye." She held out her trembling hands. "See. I'm a wreck. I just don't want to say the wrong thing." She bit her lip as her mind raced with all the things she wanted to say, all the regret she had stored up inside her. But she knew it would never be enough. It would never fully convey her profound remorse.

Holly folded her arms across her chest. Her blue eyes were frosty. "Well, anything is better than silence. That's all you've given me over the past eight years. A profound, deafening silence. And it spoke volumes, Cassidy. You've managed to avoid this face-to-face meeting for a long time."

"I know. This moment is long overdue," Cassidy acknowledged, trying to find an opening so she could make her apologies and try to bridge the gap between them.

"That's an understatement," Holly said with a harsh laugh. "We were best friends! There wasn't anything we didn't share. Hopes, dreams, disappointments. We were always there for each other. Yet when I needed you most—you bailed on me." The tone of her voice suddenly became sharp. "You should have been there! And it had nothing to do with you being the driver when the accident happened. It had everything to do with supporting me through the darkest hours of my life. Nurturing me. Holding my hand." Her voice became clogged with emotion. "I was scared—and depressed—and angry at God. Where were you, Cassidy? Where were you?"

Holly let out a hollow laugh. "Oh, yeah, I forgot. You were at art school in Phoenix."

Cassidy cringed when she heard the bitter tone in Holly's voice. It wasn't easy to face the hurt and anger head on, but she understood where the feelings came from. She'd abandoned her. Like a thief in the night she'd slipped out of town without even a single word of goodbye. For what it was worth, she could tell Holly about all that she'd been through after she left West Falls—her own fear and loneliness, the endless night terrors and the gaping hole in her heart that nothing in Phoenix could fill up. But this wasn't about her suffering. It was about making amends for the pain she'd caused Holly. It was about acknowledging that as much as she'd loved her best friend, she'd failed her on so many levels. And now all she could do was speak from the heart.

"I'm so sorry, Holly. For the accident. For what happened to you. For leaving. What I'm most sorry about is that I wasn't a better friend. I should have stuck by you. I should have been right by your side when you were in the hospital. And I should have held your hand and told you jokes and let you lean on me. Because the one thing I do know without a shadow of a doubt is that you would never have walked away from me." She clenched and unclenched her hands. "It's not that I didn't care. I did. I still do. So very much. I was just so afraid of facing charges and being arrested that I let the fear take over. I thought running away was the answer. I'm so ashamed of that."

The room was silent as Cassidy's apology settled in. Tears pooled in Holly's eyes, and she wiped a few stray ones from her cheeks.

When she spoke her voice was soft and husky, brimming with emotion. "For so long I blamed you. For the accident. For the fact that I wasn't wearing a seat belt. I think I even blamed you for the rain-slicked roads that night. Most of all I blamed you for breaking Tate's heart." She let out a harsh laugh. "I don't blame you anymore, Cassidy. I forgave you a long time ago. But forgiving you doesn't absolve you from all the hurt you caused. I'm sure you know that."

Cassidy shook her head in disbelief, unsure of whether or not she'd heard Holly's words correctly. Of all the people in West Falls, surely Holly had the most reason to harbor grudges against her. And yet she was the one offering forgiveness?

Tears misted in her eyes and she blinked them away, unwilling to give in to the emotion of the moment. "How? Why?" she asked, feeling choked-up. "I put you in that wheelchair. I should never have acted so irresponsibly that night."

"We were all irresponsible. We were all part of that stupid game. It so easily could've been me who slid off the road. Or Regina. It was just plain bad luck that it was you, Cass."

Tears streamed down Cassidy's face and she did nothing to stem the tide. Holly's words had lifted a huge weight off her shoulders. She felt lighter than she'd felt in years. Forgiveness was so much more than a word. It was a living, breathing thing. A gift from the heart.

Cassidy bowed her head. "For so many years I didn't think I was worthy of forgiveness. I still struggle with that idea. For years after the accident I didn't pray. I thought God had turned his back on me, so I turned my back on him."

Holly nodded her head vigorously. "Sounds a lot like what I went through. I came to church one Sunday after a whole year of avoiding it. What kind of God, I asked myself, would allow me to lose the use of my legs? I was lost. Broken, both literally and figuratively. And then during the service, your father started reading from Isaiah. If I live to be a hundred I'll never forget what he said." Holly's eyes were shining with emotion and she looked more joyful than Cassidy had ever seen her. "Those who hope in the Lord will renew their strength. They will soar on wings like eagles." Holly shut her eyes and bowed her head down. "I felt like he was talking directly to me. From that point on I held on to hope and I let go of all the bitterness. I'm just sorry that I didn't reach out to you to let you know. I can't imagine what it must've been like to carry all that guilt around with you."

"It's okay. When I sent you all those letters I figured you didn't want to have anything to do with me. I understood."

Holly scrunched up her forehead, confusion stamped all over her face. "Letters? I never got any letters."

Cassidy paused, not certain she'd heard Holly correctly. "What? You're kidding, right?"

"I wouldn't joke about something like that. I would have given anything to get a letter from you. A phone call. Anything."

You could've called, written, sent a text.

Tate's words came floating back to her. She'd been so crestfallen when he'd laid into her in the diner that she hadn't even challenged his accusation. She hadn't wanted to point out that she'd written Holly dozens of letters. But the truth was now coming out. Holly had never received a single one of her letters. Her words, her most heartfelt apologies had been in vain.

"Wait till I get my hands on him!" Holly snarled. "Tate has gone too far this time." She quickly wheeled herself toward the door.

"No, Holly! Don't!" she cried out. The thought of Holly and Tate going head-to-head was almost too painful to bear. A healing moment had just taken place inside this room and she didn't want it to be soiled by accusations and blame.

Holly swiveled her head around, locking eyes with her. The expression on her face was fierce, her blue eyes stormy. "I'm not letting him get away with this!" she said through gritted teeth.

Cassidy held up her hands. "Hold on a second. The Tate I used to know wouldn't keep my letters from you. Think about it, Holly. He's always had a hard time lying. Do you really think he would've been able to keep this a secret from you all this time?"

Cassidy searched Holly's face, hoping that her words had sunk in. The last thing Main Street Church needed was an irate Holly confronting Tate inside it. She knew her friend well enough to know she was fully capable of doing it.

Holly let out a deep sigh, her slight body shuddering with the effort.

"You're right. That's not Tate's style. Even when we were kids he felt bad telling a lie." She shook her head. "But if it wasn't him, then who was it? It's gonna eat me up inside if I don't figure it out."

"How can I ask for forgiveness if I'm not willing to give it myself? It doesn't really matter who intercepted the letters. All that matters is that you believe I sent them."

"I believe you. Whenever you tell a lie your face turns red and you start stammering. Remember that time in third grade when you lied to Mrs. Adams about putting the frog in Kenny Hendrick's lunch box?"

They looked at each other for a moment before bursting into giggles. The giggles became snorts until they were both holding their sides with merriment. Tears born of laughter streamed down their reddened faces.

"Poor Kenny!" Cassidy said as she swiped at her eyes with the back of her hand.

"Oh, Cassidy. I've missed you something awful." Holly was smiling as tears slid down her cheeks. "There's no one else in the world who I could laugh with over that."

Cassidy moved toward her, bending over and wrapping her arms around her in the tightest of hugs. She felt Holly squeezing her back and she held on for dear life as pure happiness flowed through her.

For forty minutes Tate had paced the aisle of the church, his movements lacking the cool, calm and collected air he usually radiated. He'd looked at his watch a dozen times or more, all the while wondering what was taking them so long.

"Will you sit down!" Regina griped. "You're going to wear a hole in the floor."

"I need some fresh air," he said as he pushed open the church doors, squinting as a blast of sunshine hit him square in the face. Regina followed closely behind him, clucking like a mother hen.

He raked his hand through his hair and filled his lungs with gulps of fresh air.

"Sorry. I'm just a little nervous about what's going on back there."

Regina rolled her eyes. "What do you think is going on? They're bonding."

He raised his eyebrows. Bonding? He hadn't imagined something as mundane as that, not after such a long separation. Not after all the heartache, betrayal and tears.

"You think?" he asked, scratching his head in confusion.

"Yup," she said, nodding her head emphatically. "No matter what's happened in the past, those two love each other. I've never seen a deeper bond. Well, other than the one you and Cass shared," she said sheepishly. "Surprised it's taken eight years to mend that friendship."

He studied her for a moment, trying to figure out where she stood in all this. "You okay with that?"

Regina's brown eyes widened. "Of course I am. Why wouldn't I be?"

"In the past you've been a bit envious of Cassidy and Holly's friendship." He eyed her warily. Regina and Cassidy's relationship had always been a touchy subject.

Regina planted her hands on her hips. "I love my cousin, Tate. I want her to be happy."

"I know you do, but in the past you've had your issues with her." He tried to be as gentle as possible with Regina, but sometimes he found it best to be direct with her.

Regina bit her lip. "Tate, I admit I was jealous. It was hard playing second fiddle to Cassidy when we were growing up." Her voice got small. "She had everything I always wanted. Most beautiful girl in town. Cheerleader. The pastor's daughter. Most of all she had two parents who loved her more than anything. That's hard to deal with when you don't feel very loved by your own parents. I'm sure I acted out at times, but I didn't know what to do with all those feelings. I've grown up since then."

"Awww, Regina," Tate said, placing his arm around her shoulder and drawing her close. His heart ached for her—he knew that being abandoned by her parents had left deep emotional scars.

Regina pushed him away. He saw her eyes welling up with tears. "Don't you dare feel sorry for me, Tate Lynch. I'm a successful Realtor with my own business, I'm pretty easy on the eyes and I dealt with my family issues ages ago!"

He held his hands up to ward her off. "Hey, you're preaching to the choir. I already know how great you are."

"Thanks for saying that," she said, a pleased smile lighting up her face. "I'm going back inside before I melt."

Everyone had their issues, he realized. Regina had spent her entire life living in her cousin's shadow while Cassidy had felt the need to run away from everyone she loved. He hadn't been able to forgive and truly forget despite a fervent desire to do so. When he made his way back inside the church he chose to stand in the back by himself. The way his nerves were jangling, he didn't think he was fit company for the Blakes.

The whirring sound of Holly's wheelchair had him turning his head in the direction of the hallway. Holly and Cassidy were making their way toward them. Both of them looked relaxed and peaceful. At the sight of them, something inside his heart shifted. Fear took a backseat. They both looked so content.

While Holly went to talk to Pastor Blake, who'd been patiently waiting in the front pew with Maylene, Cassidy strode directly toward him.

"You can stop worrying, Tate. We're both still in one piece."

"Things went well?" he asked. He asked the question as if he hadn't just been nervously pacing the aisles.

Cassidy smiled. "Very well. We talked it out. She's amazing, do you know that?" she asked. "She said she forgave me a long time ago."

Somehow it didn't surprise him. Holly had reached

a state of grace that he could only aspire to. He kept quiet, waiting to hear more about their conversation.

"We ended up laughing and carrying on about something that happened in third grade." Cassidy shook her head as if she couldn't believe how things had turned out. "It felt like we'd never been apart. I know there's still a lot of hurt there, but I'm hoping she'll let me help heal those wounds."

Tate couldn't help but smile. He hadn't realized it until just now, but he'd missed the easy friendship that the two girls had shared. It had always been filled with so much joy and laughter. And, despite his reservations, he knew that Cassidy's friendship would fill a huge, gaping void in his sister's life. That's all he'd ever wanted for Holly—to find peace in her everyday life. He envied her. Clearly, she'd found peace in forgiveness, something he still hadn't been able to achieve for himself.

"Tate, I'm sorry." Cassidy had a contrite expression on her face. Her eyes were swirling with a host of emotions he couldn't decipher.

"For what?" he asked, genuinely at a loss as to why he was getting an apology from Cassidy.

"For everything. When I looked at my day planner this morning I realized what today is. What it would've been."

He let out a sigh. Somehow he'd been hoping that no one would mention it, that he could lick his wounds in private. With Cassidy's return, he should have realized that the past would be staring him right in the face.

"Would've beens don't really count." Although his voice sounded casual, his insides were churning.

"Don't they?" she asked coolly.

He shrugged. "We didn't get married. It's not like today is our anniversary or anything."

"So you've never thought about what our lives would've been like if we had walked down the aisle?"

He fidgeted, pulling at the collar of his shirt. "Not really. I mean…of course I've thought about it. But I try not to dwell on it. No use dwelling on something that wasn't meant to be."

"I'm not trying to rub your nose in it or bring up something that you've closed a door on," Cassidy explained. "Being back home has just brought up a lot of…I guess you might call them unresolved issues. So when I saw today's date it just made me think of things I hadn't thought of in a long time."

"Everything is hitting you all at once. Your mom being sick, coming home, reconnecting with Holly." He cast her a sly grin. "And of course dealing with an ornery sheriff is never easy."

"You're not so bad," Cassidy said in a quiet voice, her eyes roaming over his face.

"For what it's worth, I'm happy for you and Holly." He shot a quick glance over at his sister, who was wildly waving her hands and beaming from ear to ear while talking to the Blakes. "It's nice to see her so content." He stroked his jaw for a moment, his eyes trained on the floor. "I have to admit, I didn't even want the two of you in the same vicinity, never mind having a one-on-one. But I was wrong about that. Holly's stronger than I give her credit for being. And the bond between you two…" The texture of his voice changed, becoming husky with emotion. "I guess it's stronger than old wounds. So, thank you, Cassidy, for giving her peace. You did that."

Without warning she threw herself into his arms, snuggling up against his chest and embracing him. The scent of her shampoo—strawberries and cream—rose to his nostrils.

"Hearing that from you means the world to me," she whispered as she nestled herself deeper into his chest. His arms rested helplessly at his sides. He wanted to wrap his arms around her, but he knew if he did he was only making trouble for himself. It was far too dangerous. Surrendering to the impulse would be like being pulled under by quicksand. When Cassidy finally let go of him and took a step away from him, he felt a nagging sense of loss. Her face was a bit blotchy from crying and she couldn't quite look him in the eye. She muttered a few words of apology.

Although he wanted to believe in her sincerity, the past crept along his spine like a spider, reminding him of all the pain she'd brought into their lives. Who's to say she wouldn't do it all over again?

"If you hurt her again you'll have to deal with me. Understand?" His words came out harsher than he intended.

With a look of hurt in her eyes she slowly nodded her head, then turned around and made her way back down the aisle toward her family and Holly.

He felt a little badly about embarrassing her. The way she'd slinked away like a wounded possum nagged at him. He wasn't used to seeing her like that. Would it have killed him to hug her back? *Yes, it might've,* a little voice in his head whispered. Did he have to rub her nose in the fact that she'd hurt Holly so deeply? *Yes! There was no point in sugarcoating things.*

What did he have to feel guilty about anyway? West Falls was just a temporary resting place for Cassidy. As soon as her mother was on the mend, she'd be returning to her life in Phoenix. It would probably be another eight years until he saw her again. Maybe she'd have a husband and some kids by then, he thought. The idea of Cassidy being married to someone else didn't sit well with him, but he knew it was bound to happen. Her future wasn't in the small town of West Falls. It was in the big, bustling city of Phoenix.

But this time when she left, as she was bound to do, she wasn't taking his shattered heart along with her.

Chapter Six

Two long weeks had gone by since Cassidy had reunited with Holly at Main Street Church. Two weeks
during which her mother had undergone her surgery—a
lumpectomy—and Cassidy had served as her primary
caregiver. Prior to the surgery, an MRI had revealed
that the chemotherapy had indeed shrunk the tumor,
leading to a less invasive procedure. The Blakes had
been ecstatic. In her postsurgical visit the doctor had
announced that the entire tumor had been extracted and
that all the remaining lymph nodes were clean. Cassidy
couldn't remember a time when she'd been more thankful for God's blessings.

At the moment all her mother had to do was rest,
gain some weight back and follow up with her doctor
at regular intervals. Although she'd been given the option of more chemotherapy treatments and radiation, her
mother had declined. Cassidy was proud of her mother.
She'd done her homework and come up with options that
she was comfortable with during her recovery.

There were so many prayers being offered up for her
continued good health and speedy recovery. A week ago

her mother had made the decision to share her health crisis with the congregation, who'd been showering her with cards, calls, meals, floral bouquets and well-wishes ever since.

Cassidy didn't quite know what to do with herself since her father had whisked her mother off to a romantic lunch date. Although she was still a bit sore at her incision site, her mother had felt well enough to venture out. Cassidy felt a pang of envy as she watched her parents walk hand in hand toward the car. Would she ever have enduring love? If she ever had a life challenge to overcome, would there be someone by her side to weather the storm?

The one thing she knew for certain was that she couldn't move forward without closing the door on the past. Although she thought she'd done that by leaving West Falls, coming home had made her realize that all she'd done was run away. That didn't give you closure. It didn't put a period at the end of the sentence.

Cassidy lifted the lid of her ballerina jewelry box and pulled out the velvet box. It was still there just where she'd left it. She shouldn't be surprised considering her parents hadn't changed a single thing about her bedroom in all these years. As a teenager she'd loved the look. The walls were still painted a light cream tone, the romantic duvet with the blue roses still covered her bed and the frilly lace curtains still hung by the two bay windows. Part of her wouldn't have blamed them if they'd transformed it into an exercise room or a sewing room. Eight years was a long time to keep the faith.

With trembling fingers she flipped the lid open. She let out a sigh as the antique diamond ring sparkled and winked at her from its velvet throne. She reached in and pulled it out. Out of force of habit she slid the ring onto her finger and marveled at how beautiful it looked.

It was the most stunning thing she had ever owned in her life. It was like no other engagement ring she'd ever seen. Problem was, it wasn't her ring anymore and it hadn't been since the day she'd ended her engagement to Tate. She had tried to return it to him before she'd left town, but he'd refused to accept it. Her parents had balked at the idea of returning it to Tate themselves. It was their belief that only she and Tate could resolve the matter. Regina had pretty much laughed in her face when she'd asked her to do it. In the end she had placed the ring in her jewelry box where it had been sitting all this time.

It's Tate's ring. He should be able to give this ring to his future wife.

The thought of another woman wearing her ring was painful. Although she wasn't in love with Tate anymore, it hurt to know he would greet another woman at the altar and make her his wife. She didn't know why it should cause her such pain, but it did. It made her ache inside. It made her question every choice she'd made over the years. Yet she knew that she still had to do the honorable thing, regardless of what it might cost her.

As Cassidy sped down the country road she let out a deep sigh as the Lynches' spectacular ranch came into view. She slowed down as she reached the massive gates, her eyes honing in on the sign welcoming her to Horseshoe Bend Ranch. Lush green acres stretched out before her, as far as the eye could see. This was Texas ranch land in all its glory, she thought, full of beauty and majesty.

Horseshoe Bend ranch had been in Maggie Benson Lynch's family for generations. Maggie was the only child of a wealthy horse breeder who'd left the rolling hills of Kentucky in order to carve out a stake for himself in Texas. Frank Lynch had been the poor cowhand who'd fallen head over heels in love with Maggie, so much so that they'd run off and eloped against her family's wishes. But Frank had proven himself, according to Tate, by transforming Horseshoe Bend Ranch into one of the most profitable horse breeding operations in the state. He'd earned the Bensons' approval through hard work, grit and determination.

Tate and Holly had inherited their parents' love of horses. On their first official date Tate had taken Cassidy horseback riding on the property, giving her one of her first tastes of freedom. He'd been raised in a saddle, and he'd taught her how to ride. Galloping across the lush Texas countryside with Tate had allowed her to become one with the horse and nature. It had been a liberating experience, one she'd never forgotten.

About a half mile from the entrance she reached a fork in the road. On her right was the main house, sitting back a ways from the road. It was a sprawling two-storey home with a wraparound porch and black shutters. The front door was painted a festive, inviting red. Brightly colored rocking chairs adorned the front porch. A hammock sat lazily between two trees in the side yard. She could see the ramp leading up to the front porch. For some reason it was jarring to see it. Handicap accessible.

Two dogs barked at her car from a distance, making quite a commotion. She didn't slow down, just continued left at the fork toward the stables. The endless acres of land never failed to move her. This perfect slice of heaven. Her eyes roamed over the vista and she marveled at its majestic beauty. She cast her gaze toward the storm clouds gathering in the sky. A squall was headed their way in the next few hours. It had been foolish to come all the way out here with a storm brewing, but she'd been determined to handle this unfinished business.

Upon approaching the stables she parked her car on the side, next to three trucks. As soon as she turned the corner by the stables, she caught sight of Tate standing next to the corral.

From across the yard she studied him—his full lips, strong jaw, the cleft in his chin. The proud way he carried himself. A cowboy hat was perched on his head. His long powerful legs were encased in a pair of dark jeans. He wore a plain sleeveless white tank. Everything about him screamed out cowboy. Even though it had been his lifelong dream to be a sheriff, being a cowboy ran deep in Tate's blood. His respect for the land, his love of horses, his rugged good looks and his strong work ethic. He was pure Texas, born and bred.

A large, bucking horse was being led out into the corral by one of the ranch hands. Cassidy watched as Tate expertly lassoed the stallion and began manipulating the horse using the rope. He was breaking in a wild horse. She'd seen it done dozens of times at this very ranch. The horse in question seemed to be giving him a run for his money.

She kept herself hidden, not wanting to provide even an ounce of distraction. Breaking in a horse was a dangerous business, even for someone who'd been doing it for most of his life. Everything could turn on a dime. The horse could kick him in the head, or Tate could get tangled up in the rope.

The stallion quieted, which allowed Tate to approach him and pat him down. His next move was to slap a saddle on the stallion and mount him. He did it with lightning speed, a blur of motion as he attempted to ride the stallion. At first the horse bucked and resisted him, at one point almost tossing him off, but Tate managed to stay on and assume control.

Tate galloped around the corral, his sturdy physique cutting an imposing figure as he sat astride the stallion. The horse was a beauty, she acknowledged. Dark as the night and full of grace and power. He had his own special language with horses. He seemed to understand them, as if by intuition, and in return they instinctively responded to him.

It was nice being back at Horseshoe Bend Ranch. It soothed a certain part of her soul. But she hadn't come out here for a social visit or to watch Tate break in a wild horse. She'd come for one reason only. To give Tate back the one thing that still tied them together.

The hot sun beat down on him as he dismounted from the stallion. He reached into his front pocket and pulled out some apple bits, offering them to the horse he'd nicknamed Rebel. Although Rebel had been nothing but trouble up to this point, he showed a rare promise that Tate hadn't come across in a long time. His father called it mojo. He called it the X factor.

What he wouldn't give at the moment for a cool glass of lemonade. He wiped away beads of sweat from his forehead, gazing up at the clouds gathering on the horizon. It was muggier than usual for this time of year. A storm was moving in, according to the National Weather Center and the local meteorologists. Although the hurricane that had ravaged parts of coastal Mexico had blown off course, Texas was still expected to get quite a wallop from a summer squall.

When he turned Rebel around, Cassidy was standing there as if she'd appeared out of thin air.

She was dressed casually in a pair of khaki shorts, a sleeveless top and a pair of cowboy boots. He knew a look of surprise was stamped all over his face. Without a word he handed the reins over to Malachi, one of the ranch hands who'd been watching him break Magic in. Malachi looked at him curiously as he made his way over to Cassidy.

"Hey! What brings you out here?" he asked, meeting her halfway between the stables and the corral.

"I'm sorry I didn't call. I figured you would tell me to stay away." She shrugged, then dug into her leather purse and pulled out the blue velvet box. He immediately recognized it, right before she said the words that made his heart run cold.

"I wanted to give you back your ring," she said in a soft voice, her green eyes somber.

She held out the box, her fingers trembling with the effort.

His heart jerked painfully as he laid eyes on it.

All the memories came flooding back to him, slicing through him with the force of a tsunami. His hands remained at his sides. He didn't think he could reach out for the ring if he tried.

"I don't want it," he said in a low voice. He could barely get the words out he was so twisted up inside. Seeing the blue velvet box was a blast from the past he hadn't expected. The last time Cassidy had tried to give it back to him had been when she'd ended their engagement. His reaction had been to slam his fist through the barn wall. All he'd felt then had been anger. Now he just felt empty.

"Here. Take it. This ring has been in your family for generations. It's only fitting that you give it to your future wife."

Ring. Future wife. The words were rolling around his head like an out-of-control train. He couldn't make sense of them.

"I never thought I'd see this thing again." Truth to be told, he'd hoped he never would. The ring represented every hope and dream he'd ever held in his heart for the two of them. When it had all crashed and burned, he'd wanted the ring to go up in smoke along with everything else.

"Take it. Please," she begged. "I've felt so guilty about holding on to this. It doesn't belong to me anymore."

"I can't take it," he whispered, his eyes rooted to the box. His nostrils flared. His breathing was uneven. Taking the ring back would be like losing Cassidy all over again. He didn't think he could go down that road again. It was too dark and twisted. Too filled with peril.

YOUR PARTICIPATION IS REQUESTED!

Dear Reader,

Since you are a lover of inspirational romance fiction — we would like to get to know you!

Inside you will find a short Reader's Survey. Sharing your answers with us will help our editorial staff understand who you are and what activities you enjoy.

To thank you for your participation, we would like to send you 2 books and 2 gifts — **ABSOLUTELY FREE!**

Enjoy your gifts with our appreciation,

Pam Powers

SEE INSIDE FOR READER'S SURVEY

For Your Inspirational Romance Reading Pleasure…

Get 2 FREE BOOKS that feature contemporary love stories that will lift your spirits and reinforce important lessons about life, faith and love.

We'll send you 2 books and 2 gifts
ABSOLUTELY FREE
just for completing our Reader's Survey!

YOUR READER'S SURVEY
"THANK YOU" FREE GIFTS INCLUDE:

▶ 2 Love Inspired® books
▶ 2 surprise gifts

PLEASE FILL IN THE CIRCLES COMPLETELY TO RESPOND

1) What type of fiction books do you enjoy reading? (Check all that apply)
- ○ Suspense
- ○ Inspirational Fiction
- ○ Modern-day Romances
- ○ Historical Romance
- ○ Humour
- ○ Mysteries

2) What attracted you most to the last fiction book you purchased on impulse?
- ○ The Title
- ○ The Cover
- ○ The Author
- ○ The Story

3) What is usually the greatest influencer when you <u>plan</u> to buy a book?
- ○ Advertising
- ○ Referral
- ○ Book Review

4) How often do you access the internet?
- ○ Daily ○ Weekly ○ Monthly ○ Rarely or never.

5) How many NEW paperback fiction novels have you purchased in the past 3 months?
- ○ 0 - 2
- ○ 3 - 6
- ○ 7 or more

YES! I have completed the Reader's Survey. Please send me the 2 FREE books and 2 FREE gifts (gifts are worth about $10) for which I qualify. I understand that I am under no obligation to purchase any books, as explained on the back of this card.

❏ I prefer the regular-print edition
105/305 IDL F5DN

❏ I prefer the larger-print edition
122/322 IDL F5DN

FIRST NAME   LAST NAME

ADDRESS

APT.#   CITY

STATE/PROV.   ZIP/POSTAL CODE

© 2013 HARLEQUIN ENTERPRISES LIMITED
® and ™ are trademarks owned and used by the trademark owner and/or its licensee. Printed in the U.S.A.
LI-SUR-13

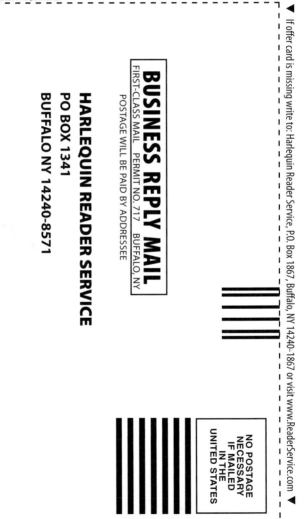

"I can't keep it." Her voice sounded agonized. She reached for his hand and tucked the box in his palm. She then folded his fingers over the box. She clasped his hand for a moment, then let go, her eyes shimmering with emotion.

He clenched his teeth. "I won't ever give this ring to another woman. It may have been in my family for generations, but from the moment I placed it on your finger, I knew it was made for you." He locked gazes with her, beseeching her for understanding. "Don't you see, Cass? All I think of when I see this ring is you."

There would always be a place in his heart carved out just for her. It was that simple. He was no longer in love with her, but she had a forever kind of place in his heart. And this diamond engagement ring represented one of the darkest chapters in his life. Having it back in his possession was yet another reminder of everything that had fallen apart.

Lord, please help me. Give me the strength to accept this ring back with the same grace that I gave it to the woman I loved.

Cassidy hung her head. "I felt so honored to wear your ring. Every time I looked at it, there was such joy in my heart. The day you gave it to me was the happiest day of my life."

He let out a deep shudder. "Mine too. I had so many dreams that were wrapped up in the two of us. I never told you this, but I already had a house in mind for us to buy. I'd already approached the Realtor about making an offer on it."

Cassidy's eyes widened in surprise. "Which one?"

"That yellow Victorian out by the swimming hole.

The one with the tire swing in the side yard and the pretty garden."

"I used to love that house," she said in a wistful voice that echoed his own feelings.

Tate just nodded, at a loss as to what to say at this point. They'd pretty much said it all.

Silence stretched between them. It wasn't an awkward silence, he realized. It felt like two people who were so comfortable with one another that they didn't need words to fill the silence. It had always been this way between them and he knew now it always would.

"I was watching you break in that stallion," she said, her gaze focused on the horses being led into the corral. One was a chestnut-colored mustang, the other a white palomino.

He turned toward her, noticing the way her eyes lit up at the sight of the horses. Somehow he'd forgotten how much Cassidy had always enjoyed being at the ranch and going riding with him. It seemed like a lifetime ago. Although she'd never been the most accomplished rider, she'd been more joyful riding a horse than almost anyone he'd ever known.

"His name is Rebel. He's all kinds of trouble, but I think he's a keeper." Tate felt a smile tugging at the corners of his mouth. "When he arrived here he was meaner than a rattlesnake, and his bite was almost as deadly. He's coming along though."

"Rebel. I like that."

"If you like him, you'll absolutely fall in love with Fiddlesticks."

"Fiddlesticks?" she asked with a chuckle. "What kind of name is that?"

Tate affected an outraged look. "Fiddlesticks is an awesome name. We're actually waiting for her to give birth to her foal. It'll be anytime now."

Malachi came running out of the stables, a frantic look etched on his face.

"Tate! I think it's almost time," he shouted. "I could use a hand in here." His handsome Native American features were pulled tight with anxiety. Without another word he raced back into the stables. So much for calm, cool and collected, Tate thought. He'd never seen his best friend move so fast.

He made a face at Malachi's retreating figure. "I better head in there before he loses his cool. He hasn't had a lot of experience with foal births."

"I should be heading home anyway." She cast a nervous glance at the sky. "There's a storm heading our way."

"Drive home safely, ok?" He couldn't help but feel protective of her.

He watched her walk toward her car, her movements easy and graceful. Before he could change his mind he ran after her, calling out her name. When she turned around he was standing there with his hands jammed into his back pockets, feeling a bit sheepish.

"Is something wrong?" she asked, her face showing concern.

"No, everything's fine. I just wondered if you might want to stay for a bit, to watch the foal being born."

He watched as she glanced up at the sky again. Although the wind had kicked up a bit, there was no rain falling and the sky was still light. The storm was still hours away.

Cassidy nodded her head and smiled. "I'd love to see the foal being born. It'll be a first for me."

Tate detected a hint of anxiety in her eyes and he wondered if it was about the approaching storm. "If you're worried about the storm, I can drive you back home later," he suggested. "And Malachi can drive your car behind us."

"No, it shouldn't be a problem. It hasn't even started raining yet."

"Well then," he said with a grin, "let's go inside before Fiddlesticks scares the stuffing out of Malachi."

The sound of Cassidy's tinkling laughter warmed his insides, making him feel as if he'd performed an amazing feat. Her eyes at the moment looked like glittering emeralds and her pretty mouth made him think of sweet kisses in the moonlight.

Whoa! He was starting to feel like one of his untamed stallions who needed to settle down. What he and Cassidy now shared was friendship, pure and simple. He couldn't let his mind go to that place, that faraway place where all his dreams lived. Those dreams were all tied up with the past. With one last look at Cassidy he ushered her into the stables and set about the business of delivering Horseshoe Bend Ranch's newest foal.

Four hours later and she and Tate were still awaiting the birth of Fiddlesticks's foal. Malachi had taken off a few minutes ago so that he could check on some of his relatives at the reservation. He was concerned that some of them wouldn't have heard about the oncoming storm and might get stuck in dangerous situations. Although he was a man of few words, Malachi's altruistic actions spoke volumes about his character. She had enjoyed watching the close relationship between Malachi and Tate—the easy laughter that flowed between them and the way they worked in sync as a team.

At the moment Tate seemed a little concerned about the lack of progress the mare was making in delivering her foal. He got down on his knees and spent a few minutes checking out Fiddlesticks. She was stretched out on her side and her legs were thrashing around. Tate was running his hand along the mare's back and massaging her spine.

"How's she doing?" Cassidy asked as Tate exited the stall, his jeans looking a little worse for wear.

"She's not laboring heavily yet, although she's sweating quite a bit. She's lying on her side, so she's probably having some contractions. I don't think she's ready to deliver this foal just yet though."

"Does Holly know about Fiddlesticks?"

"No, I haven't spoken to her today. She left town yesterday for a rehabilitation program in New York. They flew her down there as part of a scholarship she won." Tate beamed proudly. "It's quite an honor for her. My dad flew down with her since she hasn't flown by herself since…well, since the accident."

She felt a twinge of sadness that Holly hadn't shared her exciting news with her. Over the past few weeks they'd talked a few times on the phone and made plans to have lunch as soon as her mother was feeling better. She knew she shouldn't feel disappointed, since rebuilding their friendship would take time. Although they'd mended fences, it wasn't an instant fix. There was still work to be done.

"The program teaches independence to people with spinal cord injuries. It's one of the most successful programs in the country," Tate explained. "It's fairly expensive, so the scholarship was a blessing."

"She seems pretty sure of herself. I once heard the expression 'putting the able in disabled.' When I think of Holly that's what I think of."

"She projects confidence, that's for sure. But there's a lot of fear there. She still has some mountains to conquer…riding again, going on a plane by herself, dating. She used to love riding, but she's scared to death about getting back in the saddle." A deep sigh escaped his lips. "And the thought of traveling on a plane alone makes her anxious. She says that if something were to happen on the plane she wouldn't be able to save herself. She's actually suffered a few panic attacks." He shrugged. "Most women her age go on dates—to the movies, dinner, dancing…" His voice trailed off. "There hasn't been anyone special in her life since high school."

His voice sounded troubled and she longed to make him smile again. He'd always carried the weight of the world on his shoulders, seeming to care about other people's problems more than he cared about his own.

"Those things can be problematic for able-bodied people," Cassidy quipped. "And we all have fears. I was shaking in my boots my first day back in town."

Tate looked embarrassed. "Was that before or after you got an earful from me?"

"I don't blame you for being angry," she said in a quiet voice. "I expected it."

"I don't like feeling angry, Cass. It's not who I am, nor who I want to be."

"I feel like there's a but in that sentence." She knew this man so well. At one point in time she could practically finish his sentences for him. "Don't hold back. I can take whatever you have to throw at me."

"I've been so angry for so long. Since the accident. Since you left." He looked at her with wounded eyes and she felt her heart breaking all over again. "You leaving Holly like that, it was devastating. As a brother it killed me to watch her fall apart. But you leaving me like that and calling off our wedding…it broke me, Cass. As a man, it broke me right here." He thumped his fist on his chest. His shoulders were slumped, his head bowed. "It hurts my pride to even admit that."

She swallowed past the huge lump in her throat. "It hurts to know I've made you feel this way."

"I defended you, did you know that? To my family, to my friends, to everyone who mattered to me. I told them it was an accident, that it could have happened to anyone. I still wanted to marry you. I wanted to make a life with you, to forgive you, to help others forgive you. And then you took off without a word of goodbye. You bailed on us!"

She blinked back tears. "I can't change the past, Tate. No matter how much I wish I could."

His voice softened and became almost tender, as if he'd had all the wind blown out of him. "I know you're looking to make up for the past. I can't blame you for that. It must feel awful coming back to a town that doesn't quite accept you. The other day you asked me why I can't show you forgiveness? What you don't understand is that I'm trying to. I want to show you mercy. And kindness. But forgiveness. I struggle with it."

She reached out and touched his cheek, her hand brushing against rough stubble.

"You're human, Tate. It's not an easy thing. Forgiveness is something that's earned. I don't expect to earn it all at once." She smiled at him. "I consider it a major step in the right direction that we're able to sit here talking like two old friends. And you have been merciful. And you have been kind."

Tate met her gaze head-on and for a moment they got lost in each other's eyes. The energy in the stables shifted as awareness flared between them. He reached out and swept her hair away from her face, his touch full of tenderness. Strong arms looped around her waist, pulling her into his soft embrace. Somehow she'd forgotten how safe she felt in Tate's arms, how he was the only one who'd ever given her a soft place to fall. She'd missed their connection and the sense of security he'd always given her. She'd missed him.

He held her for a few moments before pulling away. She raised both of her hands and placed them on either side of his face, gazing intently into his beautiful blue eyes. *If only*, she thought, *this perfect moment could last forever.*

Tate leaned down, his face hovering over hers, his hands gripping her arms. Just as she thought he was going to place his lips over hers, he abruptly moved away. She looked into Tate' s troubled eyes—they were churning with emotion.

"I'm sorry about that," he said, a dazed expression on his face.

"You don't have to be sorry." She tried to make eye

contact with Tate, but he was looking everywhere but in her direction.

"I should never have tried to kiss you," he said in a strangled voice, his eyes full of regret.

Chapter Seven

Tate combed his fingers through his dark mane of hair. "I'm not making excuses for almost kissing you, but seeing you, spending time together…it's stirring up all kinds of emotions. I just don't want us to get carried away and then regret it later."

He made it sound as if kissing her would be a burden. A regret! Her cheeks burned with embarrassment. This was certainly the first time in her life someone had expressed regret about the possibility of kissing her. It prickled her pride and hurt her feelings at the same time. Right now all she wanted to do was make a quick exit and forget all about watching Fiddlesticks give birth. That way she could lick her wounds in private.

All of a sudden the stable doors flew open. A huge gust of wind blew inside, heralding the arrival of a figure draped in a soaking wet rain slicker. They stepped apart from each other, both acting as guilty as a fox raiding the chicken coop.

The hood of the rain slicker came down, revealing a disheveled looking Maggie Lynch. Her hair was coming undone from her bun and her glasses were fogged over with rain. Cassidy noticed she'd gotten a little rounder over the years and she was sporting a few gray hairs at her temples. Maggie had always reminded her of a beautiful china doll with her wide expressive eyes and her rounded cheeks. Nothing had changed in that regard. She was still striking.

"Tate, I came to tell you that they've upgraded the storm warning for this area. They've now issued a tropical storm warning," she announced as she ambled toward them from the doorway. "It's already raining like cats and dogs out there. I had no idea you had company."

Her eyes went wide as soon as she got close enough to recognize Cassidy. She turned to Tate, a look of confusion overwhelming her doll-like features.

"Tate? What is she doing here?" Her voice came out hardened, rough around the edges. She didn't sound at all the way Cassidy remembered.

Tate was eying his mother warily. "She came back home for a spell, Mama, to visit with her folks. I invited her to stay and watch the foal birth."

Maggie's gaze shifted back to Cassidy. She looked as if she'd had the biggest shock of her life.

Unsure of what to say or do, Cassidy's home training took over. "Hello, Maggie."

"Cassidy." Maggie nodded her head in her direction, still looking a little dazed by her presence at Horseshoe Bend Ranch. "I haven't laid eyes on you since the night of the accident when you picked Holly up at the house. The next time I saw my daughter she was lying broken and battered in an emergency room." Her tone was terse and no-nonsense. "I didn't see you at the hospital or the rehab appointments. You didn't call the house once. Holly asked about you every day for three months straight. I just want to let you know you broke all of our hearts."

"Mama! That's enough!" Tate said in a raised tone. "She's already acknowledged that she didn't do the right thing."

Cassidy reached out and placed her hand on his arm. "It's okay. She's just getting it off her chest." Shame ate at her, the same way it had dozens of times before.

"No, it's not okay." He cast his mother an angry look. "At some point we all have to move past the anger…that includes you, Mama."

"Cassidy should be making her way back home." Maggie's face was drained of color. She looked like she'd lost all her fight. "The storm has come earlier than predicted."

Cassidy walked toward the barn's entrance and looked through the partially opened door. The rain fell down in torrents, obscuring her view of the ranch. She could barely make out the corral in the distance. When had it started raining? Had she and Tate been so caught up in their own little world that they'd failed to notice the sudden onset of the storm?

She jumped as the crack of thunder boomed in the distance. A bolt of lightning streaked across the darkening sky. She looked up at the heavens, her nerves frazzled, torn between being a part of something beautiful, and fear. More than anything she'd wanted to stick around the ranch and watch the birthing of the foal. But now because she'd waited too late, she would be forced to drive home in driving winds and rain.

The very thought of it made her freeze up. It was

pouring outside now, and the wind was kicking up something fierce. Cassidy hated driving in rain-slickened conditions. Never mind a torrential downpour. It gave her the shivers, reminding her too much of the night she'd tried so hard to forget.

For so long she'd suppressed the memory. Now it sliced like a sharp knife through the hazy veil she'd placed over it. That night flashed before her eyes like footage from a movie reel.

The four roses had been enjoying a girls' night out. They'd enjoyed dinner at the Falls Diner followed by bowling at Lucky's. She'd recently gotten her license and had wanted to drive her girlfriends around in the used 4Runner her parents had given her for her birthday. For months now Holly and Regina had taken turns driving them around, since she and Jenna hadn't yet passed their road tests. Tonight she'd wanted to be the one carrying the keys and picking all the girls up and dropping them back home. It was a rite of passage she'd looked forward to for months.

There had been light rain all evening, adding a dreariness to an otherwise fun night. Once they'd finished bowling, boredom had set in. One of the girls—she couldn't remember who—had suggested they play the chicken game. They'd done it several times before. When it had been her turn she'd been a little nervous. She hadn't been used to driving in the rain. She didn't like the way the car skidded sometimes when she put on the brakes. Holly had been in the passenger seat and she'd taken her seat belt off so she could hang out the window and scream her lungs out. With the girls egging her on she'd darted between lanes, zigzagging with the car and careening out of her lane. When she'd hit a curve in the road the car had skidded, and despite her best efforts, she'd crashed into a stone wall. Upon impact she'd hit her head on the steering wheel and blacked out for a few moments. When she came to, Regina was screaming that she couldn't find Holly while Jenna was still sitting in the backseat, silent and in a dazed state. By the time the ambulance had come she'd scrambled out of the car and found Holly's body stretched out in the road about twenty feet from the car. The rest of the night had been a blur.

She'd been taken by ambulance to the hospital where she'd been diagnosed with a minor concussion. It was at the hospital that she'd found out Holly's spinal cord had been severed.

The four roses had promised to take their secret to the grave.

"Cassidy. Are you okay?"

The rich timbre of Tate's voice brought her back to the present. She shook her head to rid herself of the traumatic memories.

"I'm fine. I should get going though. It's really coming down out there." She bit her lip as she watched the rain pour down in sheets.

He gently turned her around so that she was facing him. "There could be downed trees, flooded roads. It's just too risky to take a chance like that. Once Fiddlesticks delivers her foal I can drive us to the main house. You can stay in one of the guest rooms."

Cassidy sputtered. "I don't think Maggie would approve of that plan." She glanced over at Maggie, who was in the stall kneeling next to her mare. "She hates me."

Tate's face held a rueful expression. "She doesn't hate you. Her bark is much worse than her bite. She's been holding all that in for eight years."

"I can't imagine my mom would've reacted any differently." Cassidy let out a sigh. "I just wonder when people will find it in their hearts to accept me without throwing the past in my face."

She knew she was feeling sorry for herself, but it wasn't easy dealing with rejection. Especially from someone like Maggie who she still cared about. Once the Horseshoe Bend Ranch had been her second home, a place where she'd found love and acceptance. Maggie and Frank had adored her. She'd loved them dearly in return. It was painful dealing with the ramifications of the accident and her exodus from town. It was disheartening to know that people might never accept her and forgive her transgressions.

But wasn't that part of her journey? Making amends wasn't a trivial thing. It was work, plain and simple. And in the end she might never find redemption. At least she would know she'd tried. She'd be leading with her heart instead of wallowing in fear and regret. She'd be living outside of her comfort zone and taking chances. She hadn't done that for a very long time.

And perhaps someday when she walked down Main Street she'd receive smiles instead of stares. Until then she would just have to keep laying the foundation for forgiveness, brick by brick.

By nightfall Fiddlesticks had delivered her foal, and the storm raging through West Falls was in full effect. Cassidy had called her worried parents, informing them that she'd be staying the night at the ranch. Tate's mother had already headed back up to the house. Tate was thankful for Cassidy's presence during the difficult foal birth. When Fiddlesticks had been in heavy labor he'd realized one of the foal's legs had been bent at an odd angle and impeding the delivery. His experience had helped in the process since he knew that he'd have to realign the foal's positioning in order for her to push the foal out. Once he'd done that, Fiddlesticks had easily delivered her foal.

"He's gorgeous," Cassidy cooed, once he'd cleared the foal of the amniotic sac and she was able to get a good look at him.

The foal looked just like his mama. He was the color of midnight. The only difference between the two was the white star on his forehead.

"He's something isn't he?" Tate beamed with pride. This newest foal wasn't just a miracle of nature. He was the living, breathing embodiment of Horseshoe Bend Ranch. Horse breeding was his family's bread and butter. It would be a legacy handed down to generations of Lynches.

"He sure is," Cassidy said, her voice filled with admiration. She was making sure to keep a safe distance from Fiddlesticks and her foal. He'd made a point to warn Cassidy about the perils of getting too close to overprotective mares.

"What are you going to name him?" Cassidy asked.

He thought about it for a second. "Why don't you name him."

"Seriously?" Her eyes widened in surprise. Her face lit up like pure sunshine.

"Yup. I've named dozens of foals. You stuck it out and helped me bring him into the world. And you got stranded here at the ranch in the process. It's only fitting that you have the honor of naming him." For Tate, nothing else would have felt right.

She tapped her chin. "Hmmmm…the obvious choice would be to name him something like Coal or Jet because of his dark coloring. And there's also Midnight or Trigger."

"You'd never make the obvious choice, would you, Cassidy?" he teased, feeling a lightheartedness he hadn't felt in years. He wouldn't have wanted to have shared this instant with anyone other than Cassidy. It felt like one of those moments when everything had aligned perfectly to make it happen. It was serendipity, he supposed.

"Of course not," she responded playfully. "I'm an artist. We're very creative people," she said with a feigned sniff. "We never resort to the obvious."

Tate laughed at her play acting. "Well then, lay it on me. I can't wait to hear what you've come up with."

She snapped her fingers, her face animated. "I have a great name. Picasso. In honor of my favorite artist. Something tells me there's not too many horses running around named Picasso."

Tate let the name marinate for a minute. Cassidy watched him carefully, her brows furrowed as she waited for his verdict. She began biting her lip. He thought it was adorable that she cared so much about his opinion. It was time to put her out of her misery. He grinned at her as he held two thumbs up. "That's a great name for him. I'm proud to announce the birth of Picasso. The latest greatest addition to Horseshoe Bend Ranch."

Tate reached out and placed his arms around her. He was happy she was here. He felt blessed that they were able to share this miracle together. For a moment Cassidy clung to him, her hands gripping the fabric of his shirt. She relaxed against him, placing her face in the crook of his arm. He reached for her chin, turning her face toward him so he could see her. Expressive green eyes looked back at him, filled with a challenge he wasn't sure he could resist. Just as he was about to brush a kiss across her forehead she took a step back away from him.

He looked at her, his gaze searching for an explanation. She met his eyes for a brief moment then broke eye contact, focusing instead on the stall behind him. For an instant he'd seen fear in her eyes. The thought that he'd done something to make her feel that way needled him, made him feel selfish for pushing too hard for something more than the easy friendship they'd settled into.

"Maybe we should head to the house before the storm gets any worse," she suggested, her voice sounding quiet.

He nodded in agreement, his mouth feeling as dry as sawdust. He'd wanted to kiss her. He'd wanted to throw all his regrets out the window and kiss Cassidy on her sweet lips with as much tenderness as he could muster. He wanted to take a chance and forget everything that had come before this moment. It would be a leap of faith, he knew, but every instinct was urging him to take a chance.

But Cassidy hadn't been sure. Perhaps his earlier

warning about getting carried away with themselves had worked against him. Maybe his own fears had come back to bite him.

He went into the tack room and rustled up two over-size rain slickers. Although the rain slicker was a few sizes too big for her, at least it would give her protection. As he opened the stable's door, using his body to shield Cassidy from the brunt of the wind and rain, he had to use every ounce of his strength not to get pushed back by the elements. After a few tense moments he staggered to the truck, guiding Cassidy into the passenger seat before fighting his way to the driver's side.

If he hadn't known the stretch of road like the back of his hand, the drive to the house would've been far more treacherous than it already was. Cassidy bit her nails during the entire ride. Her eyes were as wide as saucers as she stared out the window without uttering a single word. It was as if she was waiting for something terrible to happen at any moment. Fear. He knew it when he saw it. As a sheriff it was an emotion he was used to dealing with, whether it was a seven-year-old boy caught throwing a rock through a window or a thief nabbed for stealing from a cash register.

Lord, please let me help Cassidy ease her fears. Let me show her that she's safe with me. I'll never allow harm to come to her, not as long as I can help it.

As they approached the main house, Tate quickly noticed it lay in complete darkness, with the exception of a few lights glimmering from the interior. Hurricane lamps in a front window lit the porch steps, providing a beacon through the darkness. He said a silent prayer of thanks for his mother. She'd lit the way for them, making it easier to find their way home through the storm.

Once they were settled inside the house his mother came rushing out of the kitchen, a hurricane lamp clutched in her hand. Tate noticed she didn't seem at all surprised to see Cassidy. He liked to think she knew him well enough to know he would never send her home in the midst of a storm.

"Why don't you two wash up," she suggested. "I've got some chili on the stove."

Although his mother was being cordial to Cassidy, her disapproval radiated in waves. The firm set of her mouth, the taut lines around her eyes and her stiff body language were very telling. He prayed that it wasn't making Cassidy too uncomfortable.

The spicy aroma of the chili hovered in the air, causing his stomach to grumble. He patted it in anticipation. He walked up behind his mother and wrapped his arms around her, planting a kiss on her cheek.

"That's a real treat, Mama. Thank you." His mother was such a loving, nurturing soul. She'd cooked up more meals in their family kitchen over the years than he could count. While his father had been busy establishing himself as a horse breeder, his mother had chosen to be the stable force holding up their family. Whether it was baking cookies for the class party or helping him earn his Boy Scout badge, she'd always been there.

"That sounds delicious," Cassidy added. "I didn't realize how hungry I was until right now."

"Well, I made plenty. There's cornbread too, and salad." Maggie clapped her hands together.

"So go on and wash your hands so we can sit down at the table."

Within minutes they were washed up and seated comfortably at the kitchen table, a long butcher-block style adorned with a host of candles. The pot of chili sat in the middle of the table, along with a bowl of salad and generous chunks of cornbread. Considering the ranch had no power, this was quite a spread, Tate thought.

"Let's say grace," his mother suggested. She held out her hands to both Tate and Cassidy.

"May I?" Cassidy asked, joining hands with both of them.

His mother nodded her head. "Of course you may." Tate could see that his mother was still frosty toward Cassidy. Her tone was abrupt and the lines of her face were still tightly drawn. Perhaps her feelings would change if she could just remember who Cassidy was before her fall from grace tarnished her image. It was hard to hate someone you'd once loved.

He closed his eyes, bowed his head and let Cassidy's soothing voice wash over him. "Lord, please watch over the people of this community. Please show your loving mercy to all those who are seeking shelter from this storm. And please bless Maggie for lovingly preparing this meal."

"Amen," Tate said before digging into the chili. The warm savory dish immediately warmed up his insides. The rich flavor of the food was the perfect meal for a stormy night.

Never in a million years had he ever imagined that Cassidy would be sitting down to dinner with him and his mother at the family ranch. He'd thought those days were behind him. Although the situation was a far cry from perfect, considering his mother's cold demeanor, it was still progress. He looked over at Cassidy and their eyes locked. She smiled at him—a beautiful, pure smile that went straight to his most tender spot. He knew she was thinking the same thing that he'd been thinking. She looked happy to be sitting with them at the family table. As he sat there looking over at her, full of admiration for her radiant beauty, he could only hope that a small portion of her happiness was due to him.

Morning came after a night of punishing rain and high winds, bringing with it sunshine and clear skies. Cassidy had arisen at the crack of dawn, awoken by the sharp cries of the Lynches' rooster. She'd remained in bed for an hour or so, thinking about Tate and the time they'd spent at the stables. Sharing the experience with him had been wonderful. She finally felt as if she knew where he was coming from. He'd laid himself bare for her, stripping away the strong mask he wore so well. He was trying to find forgiveness for her, but struggling at it.

She knew all about struggle. It was the main reason she'd repaired her relationship with God after so many years of grappling with her faith. After years of wrestling alone with her feelings of guilt and pain, she'd finally acknowledged that she needed help. Sometimes a person couldn't find their way out of the darkness alone. She was living proof of that.

When she peered out the bedroom window she was relieved to see that Horseshoe Bend Ranch was still in one piece. Other than a few downed tree limbs and wooden slats strewn about the lawn, the storm had been kind to them. No major damage had been done.

As she made her way downstairs, she almost ran headlong into Tate, who was striding toward the staircase. He was dressed in his official sheriff's uniform, complete with the shiny gold badge. She couldn't remember him looking more handsome. He greeted her with a wide smile that reminded her way too much of lazy summer nights and afternoons at the swimming hole.

"Mornin', Cassidy. I was just about to knock on your door. I've got to head into town in a little bit to check in with the Sheriff's Office."

"How bad is the damage in town?" Although the harm to the Lynches' ranch had been minimal, there was no telling what devastation had been inflicted in town or in other portions of Texas.

"There are lots of reports of downed wires, flash floods and property damage. Some people still are without power, and there's no telling when they'll get it back."

The peal of her cell phone interrupted Tate. With a quick glance she realized it was her father on the line. She felt a twinge of guilt that she'd forgotten to call her parents this morning. Her thoughts had been so filled with the aftereffects of the storm and making her way back into town. It had totally slipped her mind.

"One second, Tate. It's my dad," she explained, quickly flipping open her phone. "Hey, Daddy. How's everything?"

She wasn't getting very good reception. Her father's

voice crackled on the line. She could barely hear him. "Things aren't so good here, Cass."

Her heart lurched. Had she heard him right? "Daddy. What is it? Is Mom okay?"

She felt Tate drift to her side. She clutched at his arm, afraid to even breathe until she heard her father's news.

"Yes, she's fine. It's the storm." The line continued to hum and crackle. "There's just no easy way to say it, Cass. The roof of Main Street Church blew off during the night. And until we can afford a new one, our congregation doesn't have a place to gather."

Chapter Eight

Tate led the way into town, followed by Cassidy in her sporty little ride. Along the way they saw people cleaning up from the storm, home owners using wet vacs to empty flooded basements, downed trees impeding roadways and a few ranchers looking for missing cattle. A few times he'd pulled over to inquire about the well-being of elderly residents and a few shut-ins. All in all, the community of West Falls had bravely weathered the storm.

He could tell by Cassidy's face that the news about Main Street Church had left her reeling. She was chomping at the bit to get back into town and meet up with her father at the church. As soon as they reached the corner of Oak and Main he could see the huge gaping hole where the roof had been. Not only was the roof completely missing, but the steeple had also toppled to the ground. It was now propped against the side of the church, split right down the middle. It was a jaw-dropping sight.

Before he could even park his truck, he saw Cassidy standing on the sidewalk gazing up at the church. Her hand was over her mouth, and she was shaking her head back and forth. He quickly got out of his car and joined her. A throng of people had gathered on the sidewalk, along with a camera crew for an El Paso news station. It seemed that everyone was taking stock of the damage.

"I can't believe this. How did this even happen?" Cassidy threw her hands in the air. "Most of the structures in town haven't even been touched by the storm. It's like the storm focused all its wrath on Main Street Church."

"I heard one of the meteorologists saying the winds were upward of sixty-five miles an hour. Those kind of winds wreak havoc." Given what had happened to the church, he felt grateful that West Falls hadn't suffered any loss of life or major injuries. It was certainly something to be thankful for when he knew other communities had suffered much greater losses.

Tate gazed up at the top of the church. This was much worse than he'd even imagined. A crew was going to have to get over here immediately and put a tarp over the missing roof. If it rained again the beautiful wooden pews and the interior of the church would be even further damaged. As it was, the damage to the interior amounted to minor water damage.

"There must have been some structural problems with the roof," he explained. "Looks like the storm blew through town and cut a path straight through this area."

He knew Cassidy was taking this very personally, but it was one of life's random events. No one could have predicted it or planned for it. Simply put, Main Street Church had been in the direct route of the storm.

The only one who knew the rhyme or reason for this was God.

Cassidy seemed to be listening to him, and he noticed she was nodding her head at all the appropriate times. But she still wasn't talking very much. He couldn't get past the wounded look in her eyes. Even though she hadn't been part of the congregation for many years, Main Street Church still had a place in her heart. A lot of it was tied to Pastor Blake and his leadership role in the church, but many of Cassidy's memories revolved around her singing in the choir, meeting Holly for the first time at Bible Class and playing Mary in the Christmas pageant. They were good, solid memories that had laid a huge foundation for her faith.

"Let's go inside and find your father." He led her by the elbow up the stairs and into Main Street Church. An eerie hush had fallen over it. Without its roof, the nave was bathed in natural light. It felt as if it had been cracked wide open. Tate wondered if the building was even structurally sound. Had the storm revealed some underlying weaknesses that needed to be brought to light?

It didn't take them long to find Pastor Blake. He was inside, standing in a huddle with members of the congregation. Some of the parishioners were openly sobbing while others were peppering him with questions about how quickly the roof would be repaired. There was a sense of urgency in their voices. He had to hand it to Pastor Blake. Despite the chaos swirling around him, he exuded a calm and steady presence. As soon as he saw them in the aisle, he excused himself and beat a path toward them.

Cassidy met her father halfway and hurled herself into his arms. He pulled her close to his chest and ruffled her hair. Tate detected a little moisture in his eyes as he watched the pastor whisper something in Cassidy's ear. Whatever it was, it made her smile. Seeing the love between father and daughter touched Tate's heart. He knew they'd been down a dark road in the past few years and that their relationship wasn't what it should be. Perhaps Cassidy's return to West Falls was providence.

As soon as he let Cassidy go, Pastor Blake reached out and shook Tate's hand. Tate could see the look of fatigue on his face. In the past few months he'd had to weather his beloved wife's illness, and now he'd been dealt this devastating blow to the church. Not that he would ever complain about it, but he'd been through the ringer. It was no small wonder that he had dark circles resting under his eyes.

"Thanks for coming so quickly. How did the ranch make out in the storm, Tate?" Pastor Blake asked, his warm gray eyes filled with compassion.

It was just like Pastor Blake to ask about the well-being of others. In the midst of his own crisis he was still reaching out to his congregation. He was still making sure the community was doing well and thriving. As he'd thought many times before, Pastor Blake was an amazing, compassionate man. He inspired Tate to do better, not only in his personal life but in his role as a law enforcement officer.

"Thankfully the ranch didn't have any major damage," Tate answered. "Matter of fact, I just checked in with the Sheriff's Office and so far there's only minimal damage being reported in town."

"I wish I could say the same for Main Street Church." Pastor Blake's gaze shifted upward to the rafters where the sun was now streaming down on them. "I have a roofing company coming back later to give me some quotes. I can't imagine how much it will cost to fix all this damage." He let out a huge sigh.

"Won't the insurance cover the storm damage?" He knew all policies were different, but most would provide coverage for this.

"Our particular policy doesn't include roof coverage," Pastor Blake answered, his mouth set in a grim line.

Cassidy let out a shocked cry. "I can't believe that. This was a storm...an act of God. It should be fully covered by the insurance company." Her eyes were flashing dangerously, and her cheeks looked flushed. She was standing with her arms folded across her chest. If the situation weren't so serious, Tate would have laughed at Cassidy's feisty stance. She looked ready to wage war against the insurance company single-handedly.

Pastor Blake shook his head at Cassidy. "I'm not letting God be the fall guy for this one, Cass. I was the one who selected the policy and the coverage. I'm the one at fault. If anyone in the congregation wants to point fingers, they should point them directly at me."

"Pastor Blake, you can't blame yourself. No one could've predicted this would happen."

Tate felt a stab of guilt. It seemed as if the pastor was expecting his congregation to call him out, perhaps based on events from the past. He knew all too well the ruckus his parents had raised eight years ago when they'd tried to have Pastor Blake removed as head of Main Street Church. It had caused a lot of strife and pain for the Blakes and had nearly torn the congregation apart. It was the only time in his life he'd ever felt ashamed of his family. And his mother's feelings hadn't changed all that much either, considering she wanted him to have nothing to do with Cassidy or the Blakes.

Pastor Blake raised his hands up. "I have no idea how we're going to afford a new roof, not to mention the steeple. It was the original steeple from when this church was built back in the 1800s. We're already mortgaged to the hilt. And all I keep thinking is that my congregation no longer has a place to worship." He shook his head in disbelief.

"Maybe you can raise a special collection to cover the costs," Cassidy suggested.

"Times are tough. West Falls has been hit hard by the recession, just like the rest of the country. Main Street Church is barely keeping the lights on as it is. We have programs to run, paychecks to write, missions to support…" Pastor Blake exhaled loudly. "We've already seen a drastic reduction in our weekly offerings. I don't think the town has much more to give."

As one of his parishioners walked past, Pastor Blake excused himself for a moment. Tate watched in humble appreciation as he wrapped his arms around the distraught woman. Within a manner of minutes he'd managed to bring a smile to her face despite the tears coursing down her cheeks.

Tate drew in a deep breath. No matter what the community needed to do to make it happen, Main Street

Church needed to raise the funds to restore itself. Even though it might be a huge undertaking, he was going to commit himself heart and soul to the restoration of his beloved church.

By the time her father rejoined her and Tate, the number of parishioners inside the church had dwindled down to a handful. Most of them were seated at the front of the church, their hands crossed in prayer. It moved Cassidy to see so many members of the congregation coming to support her father and send up prayers for the church. She'd spent the past ten minutes listening as members of the church choir brainstormed about ways to raise money for the repairs. Although she wished she could make a huge donation to the cause, she'd funneled all her savings into the gallery in order to make it a success. But she was dedicated to doing anything she possibly could to support the efforts.

"We need to have a gathering," Mona Jackson suggested, the words tumbling out of her mouth. "Not just any gathering, mind you. A coming together of the West Falls community to support the Main Street Church restoration."

Her father frowned. "Do you think the timing is right? We just held the church bazaar."

"And you saw how successful that was, right?" Doc Sampson asked. "It was jam-packed with people."

Doc was right. Everyone in West Falls had turned out to the fairgrounds for the event. It had been popular with all segments of the community—teens, seniors, married with kids. It had always been a can't-miss event. This year was no different.

"Yes, it was our largest fund-raiser to date," her father acknowledged. "It allowed us to make a sizable donation to a woman's shelter in Amarillo and get caught up with our bills."

"That shows that the community supports fund-raising efforts," she added. "And who wouldn't want to help restore the church?" Excitement was coursing through her. Perhaps Mona was on to something. West Falls was a town that came together in times of crisis to support one another. If they could just tap into that goodwill, they might just be able to raise the money for a new roof.

Her father looked wary. "I don't want the town to feel as if we're nickel-and-diming them."

"It's not nickel-and-diming if there's an urgent need for help," Tate said, glancing up at the missing roof. "I think this qualifies as an urgent need."

For the first time since she'd arrived her father broke into a wide smile.

"I think it sounds wonderful," he said. "Since it was your idea, I'm appointing you as organizer, Mona. I'm sure we can count on the church council, as well. We're going to need a lot of hands to pull this together. I'm going to make some calls this afternoon and put a committee together."

Mona did a celebratory dance in the aisle. Tate threw his head back and laughed at Mona's little jig, his rugged features appearing even more handsome in his relaxed state. Cassidy was overjoyed that her father had given the community gathering the green light despite his initial reservations.

"Count me in to help," Tate offered. "I'm sure you can count on Holly, too. In case you didn't know, Pastor Blake, she's your biggest fan. Main Street Church has always been there for her. I'm sure she'll want to reciprocate."

"Bless you, Tate. I'm very thankful for this community." Her father clapped Tate on the back. "Whenever I stumble in the darkness, I know the congregation will be there to lift me up."

Cassidy watched the wonderful rapport between the two men. She couldn't help but think that Tate would've been his son-in-law if they'd gone through with the wedding. The mere thought of it caused a strangled sensation to bubble up in her stomach. The regret that trickled through her caught her off guard.

"We need Main Street Church." He shifted his gaze toward Cassidy. "All of us."

Tate was right. This church was home. Although not all her recollections of this place were perfect, she'd built memories here that would last a lifetime. With the help of her father, her spiritual journey had begun within the walls of this church. And her faith was still growing by leaps and bounds. She was beginning to understand that it was a never-ending journey.

"It's a marvelous idea, but where would we have this gathering? In order to increase our revenue we need to find a venue that is as cost-effective as possible so as not to cut into the proceeds." Her father scratched his head, looking as stumped as she'd ever seen him.

Tate grinned wide, showcasing his pearly whites. "I think I might be able to help you out with this one."

"I'm open to any suggestions," her father said, his tone weary. "This aspect is crucial to the overall success of the event."

"How does this sound? A community gathering at the Horseshoe Bend Ranch, with one hundred percent of the proceeds to benefit Main Street Church restoration."

Her mouth swung open. She was stunned by Tate's generosity. His beautiful gesture. Emotion began to well up inside her. Her eyes filled with tears. She forced herself to stuff it down inside her so she wouldn't ruin the moment by blubbering like a baby.

Dear, sweet, amazing Tate. A heart as big as Horseshoe Bend Ranch.

"Oh, Tate. I can't think of a more beautiful setting. Acres of land. Wide open spaces." She clapped her hands together as ideas began to form in her head. Before she got ahead of herself with the details, she needed to get something straight with Tate. "Are you sure your parents will be okay with this?"

Hosting an event at the ranch would be a huge undertaking. The Lynch family would be the unofficial hosts of the community event, standing side by side with her father, the man they'd tried to oust from the church. She also knew that the Lynches were very private people who had withdrawn a bit from the community after the accident. Would they even allow this event to take place at the ranch? Would Maggie welcome her and her family on to her property?

Under the circumstances she wanted to be as diplomatic as possible. She didn't want to insult Tate or his family, but she couldn't ignore the huge elephant in the room.

"I don't want to bring up ancient history, but there was a point in time when Maggie and Frank were waging war against my father. If they had their way he wouldn't still be leading Main Street Church. Do you think they'll try to stand in our way?"

Tate didn't even flinch. "A fourth of that ranch belongs to me. Another fourth to Holly. There won't be a problem with hosting the gathering at Horseshoe Bend Ranch, Cass. You have my word on that."

He was standing there with his arms folded across his chest, as strong and solid as a marble statue. She had no choice but to put her faith in him. He'd never once given her a reason not to. As always, Tate was as good as his word.

"Instead of a set ticket price, maybe people will be asked to contribute only what they can afford to pay," Cassidy added. "I think that's fair." That way no one would be excluded from the gathering.

"That's a wonderful idea. That way people who are hurting financially can still come," Mona said in an exuberant voice.

"It won't matter whether they give five dollars or fifty," Doc added, a huge grin breaking out on his face.

"I'd like to add that the timing of this coincides with the church's anniversary. Main Street Church has been standing for two hundred years. Perhaps we could tie that in with the gathering," her father suggested.

"That's a great idea," Tate said. "By emphasizing how long Main Street Church has been around it really forces folks to realize how important it is to the community."

"I was also thinking that I could paint with the kids at the gathering. I could show them different art techniques that I've learned over the years." Cassidy threw her idea out there, feeling a bit uncertain as to how it would be received. She knew certain people in town didn't view her favorably. And it wasn't as if she lived here anymore. Would folks even view her as part of the West Falls community? It didn't really matter, she realized. She wanted to do something to support them. She wanted to be able to help Main Street church. And teaching kids how to paint was something she'd always dreamed of doing.

"Cassidy, the kids would be thrilled," Mona cried out.

Tate shook his head at her, his eyes filled with a mysterious look she couldn't quite put her finger on.

"What?" she asked. "Don't you like the idea?" She was practically holding her breath waiting for him to answer. She didn't know why it mattered so much to her, but she cared deeply about his opinion. With a single word he could lift her up or crush her.

"I love the idea. I was just thinking that West Falls has no idea what you could do for this town. With your huge heart and creativity, you could really whip this place into shape."

Tate's warm praise lifted her spirits even higher. Although she'd come back home to tend to her mother, she'd thought a lot lately about being in West Falls for a higher purpose. She knew God worked in mysterious ways. Perhaps she was standing in the very place she'd been meant to be this whole time.

Tate practically had to drag himself away from Main Street Church. He was on the clock now, and he felt obligated to head to the Sheriff's Office to relieve some of his deputies. Cullen had stepped up last night by riding out the storm there. He'd actually driven out during the downpour to help out one of the locals who'd been trapped in a stalled car off the Interstate. As far as Tate was concerned, he'd earned his stripes last night.

Strangely enough, all he could think about was Cassidy. Beautiful, sweet Cassidy. Somehow he'd forgotten that she had a heart as big as the great outdoors. It had been convenient to forget all the wonderful things about her and focus on the negative. It had been a survival technique, he realized. In order to get through the most painful ordeal of his life he'd chosen to think of her in purely negative terms. That way he wouldn't be tempted to miss her...to follow her to Phoenix and beg her to take him back.

Reckless. Unfeeling. Cruel. Disloyal.

He knew now that those things he'd thought about her weren't true. Cassidy had been little more than a teenager at the time of the accident. At eighteen years old she'd been scared and traumatized and vilified by the community she adored. Sheriff Keegan had even issued a warrant for her arrest. Who wouldn't have run away from all that? Who wouldn't have wanted to make a fresh start in a town where their name wasn't mud?

It was clear to him what was happening. There was no point in fighting it. He could feel the cloud lifting over his heart. For so long he hadn't even been able to think about Cassidy without bitterness welling up inside of him. Now, she was all he could think about. Dream about. And he was finding it very difficult to imagine West Falls without her, although he knew it was only a matter of time before he'd have to say goodbye.

* * *

Cassidy spent most of the morning at Main Street Church with her father. After Tate headed to the Sheriff's Office, her father led her down the hall to his private office and shut the door. He ushered her to a chair then leaned against the back of his desk with his legs crossed. He steepled his hands in front of him, a thoughtful expression etched on his face.

"Before we get started on new business, I think we have some unfinished business to settle."

"Unfinished business?" Cassidy frowned. She didn't have a clue what he was talking about.

Her father raised an eyebrow. "Your mother told me you think I'm ashamed of you."

The accusation was thrown out there like a stick of dynamite. Although she'd felt that way for years now and she'd said as much to her mother, she hadn't expected to be hashing out the issue with her father. The topic had been avoided like a live grenade for all these years—she didn't know how to tackle it. All she had were her truths.

"That's what it seems like," she admitted in a quiet voice.

He reached out to her, patting her hand in a comforting gesture. "That's not possible. You're the best thing that has ever happened to me. And you've always made me proud."

"Until the accident," she said bluntly.

"The accident—" He let out a deep sigh. "It was a low point in all our lives. I'd be lying if I said I wasn't disappointed in what happened that night, mainly because you had no business driving your friends around as a newly licensed driver. What I've learned most from that time is that we're all human, we all stumble."

Tears pooled in her eyes and she let out a shaky laugh. "All this time I thought you were ashamed of me."

He gazed into her eyes and what she saw there was regret. "I haven't communicated with you very well since the accident, but I suppose I've been dealing with my own shame."

She wrinkled her brow. "What do you have to be ashamed about?"

"Cass, you're not a parent, but trust me, when the time comes you'll do anything to protect your child. Coming up with the plan to send you to Phoenix was born out of fear. It had nothing to do with shame or disappointment. It had to do with protecting my only child." Tears misted in his eyes. "On a daily basis I tell my parishioners to face things in their life head on, but when it mattered most I did the very opposite." Her father hung his head. "If it hadn't been for me, you and Tate would be settled down into a nice life right about now."

Her father's words stunned her. All this time he'd been beating himself up about the decisions he'd made on her behalf, ones that had been motivated by love. Much like herself, he'd been mired in guilt.

"You can't blame yourself for choices I made, especially about Tate. I wanted to leave. I'm ashamed to admit this, but I felt relieved when I got to Phoenix. I was so afraid in the days after the accident. Leaving West Falls allowed me to have a fresh start."

"And now? Are you at peace, Cass?"

"Not completely," she acknowledged. "To borrow your expression, I still have some unfinished business with Tate. And I want to show the people here in town that I've done my best to make amends. Maybe then I'll be at peace."

He reached out and touched her cheek. "I'm here if you want to tell me about it. I'm a pretty good listener. And so is God. Don't forget to lean on him in times of trouble. He's always there for us."

"I know. I've said so many prayers I think God might be sick of me."

He smiled down at her, his gaze filled with compassion. "He'll never get tired of hearing from you." Like she'd done so many times since she was a child, she threw herself against his chest and found herself surrounded by his strong, loving arms. For a few moments her father gently rocked her in his arms, providing a safe harbor amidst all the uncertainty.

After their heart-to-heart, they got straight down to business. They talked with the insurance company by phone, met with a contractor and made dozens of phone calls to spread the word about the gathering. The contracting company was owned by Jim Tuggles, her high school classmate. Jim put in a reasonable bid and vowed to get the new roof put up in record time. They spoke by phone with a steeplejack—a craftsman who repaired steeples—and made an appointment for him to come see the steeple and give them a quote for its repair. Based on his comments, they soon realized that the restoration of the steeple was not a quick fix. It might take years and a great deal of money to restore it to its former glory.

By the time lunch rolled around, they'd both earned a little reprieve. They'd been working nonstop all morning. The past twenty-four hours had been a whirlwind for Cassidy and it was all beginning to catch up with her.

"Daddy, would you mind if I went out for a bit? I think I might call Regina and see if she can meet me for lunch." She and Regina were way overdue for a get-together. Regina was also on her list of people she wanted to volunteer to help with the gathering. With her professional contacts and client base, Regina could really help get the word out about restoring the church.

He smiled down at her. "Of course I don't mind. There's nothing that would make me happier than if you and Regina became close again." He glanced at his watch. "Matter of fact, I think I'll scoot over to the house and have lunch with your mother."

Within five minutes she'd made plans to meet her cousin for lunch at the Falls diner.

Twenty minutes later when she entered the diner she was greeted once again by Robin. This time the waitress greeted her like an old friend.

"Cassidy, welcome back," she said with a huge smile. "Booth or table?"

"Hi, Robin. I'm actually meeting my cousin—"

"Yeah, she's here already. She's sitting right over there." Robin jerked her thumb in Regina's direction. Cassidy's gaze shifted toward the back of the diner. Regina was seated at a booth—the same one by the jukebox where the four roses had always held court. Seeing her cousin sitting there was like taking a step back into the past. Memories as sweet as a light summer rain washed over her, making her feel like a teenager again. It put an extra spring in her step.

As she sat down at the booth, Robin placed two menus on the table, popping her gum as she recited the lunch specials and took their order. A few minutes later she returned, bringing with her two tall glasses of lemonade.

As Robin headed back to the kitchen, Regina said, "God bless Doc for giving his granddaughter a job at his diner. She's something else."

Cassidy nearly sputtered on her lemonade. "Granddaughter? She's Doc's granddaughter?"

"She sure is. Robin and her mom moved here about six or seven years ago after her parents got divorced. She's a nice girl, but quite the firecracker. Keeps Doc on his toes."

Regina stopped talking long enough to take a sip of her lemonade. After one sip she puckered her lips before dumping two packets of sugar into the glass. She swirled the contents around with a spoon then took another sip. She let out a satisfied sigh.

"I'm so glad you called me for lunch, Cass, although I'm a bit surprised." Regina bit down on her lip. "I haven't exactly rolled out the red carpet for you since you've been back."

"It's okay. We've always had an up and down relationship," Cassidy said. "When we were growing up we were more like sisters than cousins, including the whole sibling rivalry thing. But ever since I left we haven't had much to do with one another."

A look of sadness passed over Regina's face. "Cass, I

don't think you realize how much things changed when you left. I lost you, Holly and Jenna all at once."

She furrowed her brow. "What are you talking about?"

"You were the center of the friendship. When you left it all fell apart. Within a few months the three of us weren't even speaking."

Cassidy's mouth swung open. This whole time she'd assumed that the three other roses had continued their friendship without her. It was shocking to find out that it had all collapsed in the aftermath of the accident. She reached out and clasped hands with Regina. Compassion rose up within her for her cousin.

"I'm so sorry. That must have been hard for you to lose all of us at once."

Regina shrugged. "I guess you went through the same thing, huh?"

"Pretty much. But I've learned a lot about loss over the years. It's something all of us go through at one point or another. I just came from the church, and the congregation is devastated about the loss of the roof. Somehow I can't help but think that there are other communities that lost lives in this storm. There's no loss greater than that." Cassidy knew she'd be adding those lost souls to her prayers tonight.

"How is Uncle Harlan handling this crisis? I'm sorry that I won't be able to swing by and see him until this afternoon."

"He's doing as well as can be expected. First and foremost, he's holding up the entire congregation. He's dried more tears this morning than he's probably done in twenty-five years. He's like the Rock of Gibraltar, which makes me worry about him." At times like this Cassidy often wondered who her father turned to when everything around him seemed to be falling down. She smiled, knowing with a deep certainty what her father would say in response to that question. He'd quote Isaiah, as he always did, saying "The Lord God is an everlasting rock."

"That doesn't surprise me at all," Regina said. "He's always been the one to lift everyone else up even when his own soul is weighed down."

Out of nowhere a petite blond woman showed up at their booth, both hands planted on curvy hips, a warm smile enhancing her delicate features.

"Sorry to interrupt, Regina, but I just wanted to stop by and say hello to Cassidy!" The woman's bubbly voice was loud enough to turn heads at neighboring tables.

Cassidy discreetly gave her the once-over, from the top of her newly dyed hair to the soles of her high heeled feet. She looked vaguely familiar, but she couldn't place her in any memory, either from childhood or adolescence. With her long blond hair, almond-shaped eyes and trendy outfit, she was attractive in a very polished way. Despite the niggling feeling that she knew her, the woman's identity eluded Cassidy.

Before she could say a word, Regina stood up from the table, rising to her full height of five feet ten inches. She enveloped the woman in a tight hug.

"Goodness. I haven't seen you in ages, Kit," Regina gushed. "Where have you been hiding?"

Kit made a face. "Might as well have been under a rock. I've been up to my elbows in legal briefs. For once I actually had more clients than I had time to represent."

Kit. Kit Saunders? No, it couldn't be! Cassidy vaguely remembered her from high school. She'd been very overweight, always dressed head to toe in black and tended to be a recluse. The glamorous woman standing before her bore no resemblance to that frumpy girl. Her transformation was staggering.

Kit glanced over at Cassidy, a pretty smile lighting up her face. "It's nice to see you back in West Falls."

Cassidy returned the smile. Something eased inside her chest. It felt so nice to be treated like an old friend. "Thanks, Kit. It's nice to see you again, too."

"How long are you staying in town?"

"Until the end of the summer. Then I'm headed back to Phoenix."

Saying it out loud gave her a reality check. Even though West Falls was feeling more like home each and every day, it hadn't been her home for a very long time. Soon she'd be returning to Phoenix and the life she'd so carefully built for herself.

"Well, please tell your folks I said hello," Kit said in a chirpy voice. "Enjoy your summer."

After Kit left their booth and headed to the exit, Cassidy shot Regina a look of disbelief.

"I'm not trying to be rude, but wasn't she two hundred pounds or so?" The memory of a heavy-set, sullen Kit popped into her head.

Regina nodded her head. "Yeah. Incredible, isn't it? She went on some weight loss program and lost sixty pounds."

"She looks great," Cassidy acknowledged. "Wow. I would never have recognized her."

"She and Tate dated for two years," Regina said matter-of-factly.

Cassidy felt as if her heart was being squeezed inside her chest. *Two years?* Tate had dated that sweet, gorgeous woman for two years? She could feel her face dropping, but despite her best efforts she couldn't hide her dismay. It wasn't as if she'd expected Tate to never date again, but hearing that he'd been in a long-term relationship with Kit was like pouring acid in a wound.

"What's wrong? Did I say something wrong?" Regina asked, her brown eyes nearly bulging out of her head.

"Two years is a long time." Cassidy's mind began to swirl with random images. Tate horseback riding on his ranch with Kit and spending lazy afternoons at the swimming hole with her. Tate placing soft, tender kisses at the nape of Kit's neck. She closed her eyes tightly, willing the painful images to disappear.

"Cassidy, you and Tate have been over for a long time." Regina looked at her curiously. "Unless…are you and Tate back together?" She lowered her voice to a whisper. "Are you still in love with him?"

"No, we're not back together, Regina. We've been spending time together here and there—"

"And? Get to the good stuff!" Regina was leaning forward in the booth, her eyes wide with excitement. "C'mon, Cassidy." She let out a tortured groan. "I have no love life of my own. Please let me live vicariously through you, if only for a few minutes."

"And nothing. We've reestablished our friendship. He's been really kind to me, considering everything that's happened in the past."

Regina's jaw dropped. "Friendship? After everything the two of you shared you expect me to believe that you're just friends?"

Cassidy sighed, knowing Regina might never understand where she was coming from. Her relationship with Tate was filled with complexities. "Before I came back to West Falls he was nothing more than a memory, something I tried to stuff down because it hurt too much to face it. Sometimes I thought about the past and about being engaged to him, but I never really thought about him. It made it easier to leave it all behind." She let out a soft chuckle. "I'd forgotten how wonderful he is, Regina. He makes me laugh. And he's so generous. Even though he's still hurt about my ending our engagement, he still shows me kindness. Isn't that what a friend would do?" Cassidy bowed her head as sadness threatened to overwhelm her. "But he doesn't trust me yet, maybe he never will. I burned a lot of bridges with him when I left town."

"Bridges can be rebuilt, Cass. You just have to put in the hard work and be patient."

"Maggie made it clear that she doesn't want me in the picture. She can barely stand to look at me. How can I rebuild my friendship with Tate when Maggie is dead set against it?"

Her feelings for Tate were leading her in a direction much stronger than friendship, but she wasn't ready to share that with Regina. She was heading into scary territory with Tate, and she knew that with one false move she might fall headlong over the edge. Falling might feel nice, but landing with a thud would hurt.

"Cassidy, please don't take this the wrong way, but…

it sounds like if you're not careful, you're going to fall right back in love again with Tate." Regina's voice was laced with sincerity. Her eyes showed compassion and a genuine love for her cousin that Cassidy hadn't seen in years. Clearly she was looking out for her best interests.

She truly appreciated the fact that Regina cared enough about her to caution her. But she knew deep down in her soul that Regina's warning had come far too late. She was already falling head over heels in love with her ex-fiancé.

Chapter Nine

Horseshoe Bend Ranch had been transformed into a vibrant upbeat venue. Twinkling lights had been placed at the entrance to the ranch, providing a festive vibe. Red lanterns lit the road toward the main house. Tables had been set up all around the perimeter of the house, with a stage and a dance floor in the center. Teenaged volunteers, decked out in jeans and white shirts, were making the rounds with mouthwatering appetizers and sparkling cider.

Tate's parents were both dressed in their finest Western gear. Getting his father to attend the event had taken a lot of persuasion, but with Holly's help, he'd gotten the job done. His mother on the other hand had become excited once she saw her daughter's enthusiasm. She'd taken great pains to select the perfect outfit even though the event had been billed as come as you are. She'd taken Holly on an overnight shopping trip to Amarillo. They'd come back to the ranch the next day loaded down with shopping bags from cowboy boot shops and designer outlets. Tate couldn't remember the last time they'd shared such a bonding experience.

Tate studied his parents from a discreet distance. They looked scared. His father was yanking at his collar while his mother kept casting nervous glances around her. He suspected it stemmed from their uncertainty about how the congregation would receive them after the uproar over Pastor Blake. It didn't help matters that they had stopped attending services at Main Street Church. He scratched his head. For the life of him he couldn't remember the last time his parents had gone to church. It wasn't his place to judge, but everything inside him was telling him that they would thrive by being part of the congregation.

Dear Lord. Please help my parents find their way back to you. Let them rejoice in being part of a warm and loving congregation. Let them find fellowship and welcoming arms.

He wanted nothing more for them than to find everlasting peace and healing.

Tonight was a big step for them, he acknowledged. Putting their pride aside and agreeing to host the gathering had been a monumental leap in the right direction. At first his mother had been adamantly opposed to it and she'd accused him of being wrapped around Cassidy's little finger. Her venom toward Cassidy took him by surprise. His mother wasn't a vengeful woman, yet she still hadn't found it in her heart to let go of her hostility.

"The gathering isn't about Cassidy, Mama," he'd told her. "It's about coming together as a united community to restore Main Street Church. It's about stepping forward and pitching in as a town."

"Do you expect me to just forget the past?" she'd shouted, tears streaming down her face.

"No, Mama," he'd said in a subdued voice. "I expect you to do what you've always taught Holly and I to do." He inhaled deeply through his nose. "The right thing. Sometimes that's the hardest thing in the world to do, but it doesn't mean we still shouldn't do it, does it?"

In the end, after much hand-wringing and tears, she'd agreed to host the community gathering. His father had eventually relented after an emotional appeal from Holly, but he'd made it clear that he didn't want his wife unsettled by Cassidy's presence at the ranch.

Cassidy. He felt her presence before he laid eyes on her. A prickle ran down the back of his neck, and he turned around, just in time to see her striding toward him. She was decked out in a beautiful aqua shirt. An intricate pair of turquoise Native American earrings hung from her ears. She was wearing a pair of silver cowboy boots that peeked out from the hem of her jeans. Silver and blue bracelets were stacked on her wrists. All he could manage was a simple hello. The sight of her took his breath away. His mind took flight, and suddenly he was thinking of things he'd let go of years ago. He fisted his hands at his sides, resisting the impulse to reach out and wind one of her strawberry blond curls around his finger.

"Wow. Everything looks amazing!" Cassidy said, her face lit up with joy as she glanced around the area. "It is so beautiful!" Tate's eyes swept over her. The same thing could be said about Cassidy, he thought. She projected an image of classic beauty in her trendy attire.

Her subtle makeup enhanced her features, adding drama to her already striking cheekbones and eyes.

"Can you believe it? It doesn't even feel like my family's ranch." Led by Mona, he and Cassidy, along with a team of volunteers, had spent all day setting up the ranch and transforming it into a dazzling wonderland. The finishing touches—lights, sunflowers on every table, food, music—had all been added after Cassidy had gone home to change for the event. The best part was that almost 100 percent of the items had been donated by local vendors.

"The band sounds great, doesn't it? I can't believe Tug agreed to do this free of charge." Cassidy was swaying back and forth to the beat. It made him want to take her by the hand and pull her onto the dance floor. It made him want to place his arms around her and gently glide her across the floor to the rhythms of Tug Matthews and his band.

"He's just a hometown boy who wants to help out," Tate said, a smile splitting his face wide open.

A thoughtful smile hovered on Cassidy's lips. "Where you're from never leaves you. You can try to outrun it, but it always catches up to you in the end."

He felt worry gnaw at him. Would Cassidy always be outrunning her past in West Falls?

"Is that what you tried to do, Cass? Outrun it?"

"In some ways," she answered thoughtfully. "But you can't run from something that's already lodged so deeply in your heart. It would be pointless." Was he being self-absorbed or was Cassidy talking about more than West Falls now? Was there also a permanent place in her heart for him?

One of the teenaged servers walked by carrying mini beef sliders. Both Tate and Cassidy helped themselves to the appetizer. Cassidy nibbled at it delicately while he popped the whole thing into his mouth, letting out a groan at how good it tasted. She laughed out loud at his exaggerated eye roll and the way he rubbed his belly in appreciation. The sound of her laughter nudged at his heart and filled his soul with joy.

His parents appeared out of nowhere, instantly wiping the smile off Cassidy's face. Her complexion looked pale. The expressive green eyes radiated panic. Although she must have been prepared for this moment since she was standing on Lynch property, it had clearly taken her by surprise. After shooting Cassidy a look of disgust, his mother let go of his father's hand and stormed off toward the house.

His father stared after her and let out a great sigh. Considering his father's over-the-top personality and no-nonsense manner, the moment was fraught with peril. It didn't take much to imagine his father castigating Cassidy about ruining his son's life and breaking off their engagement. A dramatic scene would ruin the event they'd all worked so hard to plan. It would also further alienate a community that was just beginning to accept Cassidy.

"Cassidy," his father said in a gruff voice. "It's been a long time."

"F-Frank." All she could do was stutter his name. She was scared, Tate realized. Her hands were trembling. It took every ounce of will he possessed not to place his arm around her, pull her into the crook of his arm and shelter her from his father's wrath. But he knew that Cassidy didn't want his protection. Not now. Not in this moment. This moment had been years in the making. He knew it was part of her journey to face it down on her own, without him shielding her from it.

"It's been so long I'm surprised you still know my name," his father chided. "Eight years is a mighty long spell to be away from home." His father's unwavering gaze was locked on Cassidy.

"It's been a long time," Cassidy said with a nod of her head. "I left for the wrong reasons, Frank—the same reasons that kept me away all this time. I'd like to think that coming back was the right thing to do. It's allowed me to try and repair some of the damage I did."

Frank chewed on the inside of his cheek for a moment, his eyes narrowing to thin slits as he sized Cassidy up. "You were like a member of our family. It cut like a knife when you ran off like that."

"For what's its worth, I'm truly sorry for everything. And I'm grateful to this day for the fact that you opened up your home and your hearts to me."

For a moment they all just stood there as Cassidy's poignant words hovered in the air.

"Are you just going to stand there, or are you going to give an old man a hug?" his father barked. A huge grin split his face wide open. His blue eyes were glassy with emotion.

Cassidy reached out and wrapped trembling arms around his father, receiving a tight bear hug in return. He heard his father saying in a low voice, "I missed you, girl," as Cassidy openly wept. He didn't consider himself an emotional person, but the sight of them showing each other so much unconditional love reached down into a sacred place inside him. It tugged at him hard, cracking his heart wide open.

Even though he'd steeled himself against it, armed with the knowledge that Cassidy would soon be nothing more than a memory, he found himself surrendering to the heady pull of emotions that only she could evoke.

"I'm having so much fun." Holly's face was flushed from taking a spin on the dance floor. Her gold cowboy boots looked like something a famous country singer might wear for a photo shoot. A pair of glittery earrings dangled from her ears while her sleek chignon was a departure from her usual wild mane of hair. She was wearing a sparkled tank top and a pair of dark jeans.

"This is shaping up to be a night to remember," Cassidy said as her eyes roamed over the large gathering of people. She hadn't seen Tate in what felt like an hour, although she knew it couldn't have been more than fifteen minutes. After the reunion with Frank she'd needed to use the ladies room to fix her eye makeup. When she'd returned to the festivities Tate was nowhere to be found. Where was he?

"Looking for anyone in particular?" Holly asked, her blue eyes twinkling with mischief.

Her eyes met Holly's piercing gaze, and she felt her cheeks burn with embarrassment. Her friend had just busted her in the act of scanning the crowd for Tate.

"No one in particular," she said, unable to keep a straight face when Holly narrowed her eyes and gave her the once-over. She'd never been able to fool her best friend, not a single time. And more than anyone else, Holly had always known the strong love she'd felt for

Tate. "Okay. You caught me. I was looking for Tate," she admitted. She shook her head when she saw the flash of interest in Holly's eyes. "Don't get the wrong idea. We're just friends. Or at least we're taking steps to rebuild our friendship."

"There's a lot of water under that bridge." Something in Holly's voice sounded wary, skeptical even. Although Cassidy tried to brush it off, her feelings were slightly bruised. Perhaps Holly didn't think she was good enough for her brother.

"You're right," she acknowledged. "We've got rushing rivers between us. I did a lot of damage when I left him and he's still carrying around some of those scars." Although it pained her to think of strong, proud Tate as scarred, she knew it was the truth.

"Just tread carefully. Tate is one of the strongest men I've ever known, but his tender side makes him vulnerable, especially when it comes to you, Cass."

"Nothing I do can ever make up for the past. But I'd like to think I've grown as a person since then. If the same thing happened today I wouldn't run away from West Falls." She looked at Holly, feeling a bit defiant. "I'd stay and fight for my life."

Holly let loose with a wild hoot of laughter. "Now that's the Cassidy I know and love." Holly high-fived her and sped back onto the dance floor, spinning her chair to the music.

As she watched Holly a wave of sadness flitted through her. She hadn't divulged the whole truth to her. The real truth was that she was more likely than Tate to get her heart broken. Her feelings for Tate were getting more intense each and every day. To her it felt much deeper than friendship. It felt as if her heart was finally coming back to life after years of being in hibernation. But with the truth of the accident standing between them she couldn't even allow herself to hope. If Tate knew the real reason she'd skidded off the road that night, he'd hate her forever. And so far she hadn't been brave enough to divulge the truth to him. She doubted whether she ever could.

A sense of accomplishment filled her as her eyes swept over the teeming crowd. The gathering was a success in every way imaginable—financially, socially and spiritually. The community of West Falls had turned out in droves to support the restoration of Main Street Church. Folks from neighboring communities had also showed up, dressed in their finest Western gear with cash in hand. It spoke to how deeply people cared about the church—and her father.

Her parents were dancing cheek to cheek, and she studied her mother for signs of fatigue. Surprisingly her mother's energy level seemed good. She still hadn't put back on enough weight, but the doctors were incredibly pleased with her progress. *Dear Lord, thank you for your many mercies and for watching over Mama during her illness. I promise to be a more permanent fixture in my parents' lives. I promise to care for them as they've always cared for me.*

Her mother's cancer diagnosis had shown her that tomorrows are never promised. For years she had made the mistake of taking her parents for granted, firm in the belief that they would always be there. Seeing her mother weak and vulnerable in the recovery room after surgery had shown her the stark truth. Although her parents were superheroes in her eyes, in actuality they were mere mortals, susceptible to illness and aging and all the things life threw at people. They wouldn't be around forever.

Cassidy prayed she would never forget that again. Every day with her parents was a gift.

Mona Jackson was wildly waving from the dance floor, beckoning her to come join her and her partner. Cassidy smiled at her joie de vivre. Mona really knew how to live life to the fullest. Without her inspiration, this event would never have gotten off the ground. Jim Tuggles and his heavily pregnant wife, Candace, were seated at one of the tables chatting with another couple who were also expecting a baby. Cassidy, who'd always nurtured dreams of having a house full of infants, couldn't help but think that these couples must be the most fortunate on earth. What must it be like, she thought, to be so blessed?

When she turned back around to rejoin the party she came face-to-face with her past.

Jenna Keegan, with her caramel-hued eyes, jet black hair and café-au-lait colored skin looked as striking as ever. She had always been exotic and beautiful, Cassidy remembered, even as a child. The ensuing years had only served to enhance her beauty. Tonight the peach and silver blouse she wore looked lovely.

As a teen Jenna had been shy and reserved. She'd struggled with fitting in, largely due to her biracial heritage. Her mother's mysterious disappearance hadn't helped things any. It had only served to make her feel more different and isolated. Her friendship with the three other roses had finally given her a place to belong.

"Hello, Cassidy." Jenna nodded her head imperceptibly, her voice sounding formal and polished. There was no spontaneity in her greeting, no joy at seeing an old friend.

"Jenna. It's so good to see you." She meant it. Although the years had stretched out without them sharing even a single conversation or email, Jenna still held a special place in her heart. Hadn't they always promised to be forever friends?

There was no warmth in Jenna's eyes. When Cassidy reached out to hug her, it felt like she was touching a marble statue. Her posture was straight and rigid, her arms never moved from her sides.

"I heard you were back," Jenna said in a flat voice, causing Cassidy to wonder whether she thought her return was a good or bad thing.

"Yes, I've been back for over a month now. My mother's been sick. I've been helping her recuperate," she explained. By this time most of West Falls had heard about her mother's breast cancer diagnosis. It was no longer a closely guarded secret.

Jenna's face softened. "I didn't know she's been ill. I really hope she gets well soon. Your father may be the heart of Main Street Church, but your mother is definitely the soul of it."

With a sliver of a smile and a small wave of her hand, Jenna ambled off, her long wavy hair blowing in the breeze. A wistful feeling fluttered through Cassidy. She wished they could have really talked, not just exchanged pleasantries.

Tate came striding toward her, pausing along the way to greet guests or to direct one of the servers in a task. His blue eyes radiated a warmth that came straight from his soul.

He looked so handsome tonight. With his midnight-colored shirt, freshly cut hair and a rocking pair of cowboy boots, Cassidy couldn't help but stare at him. The black Stetson added a touch of mystery to his ensemble. She hadn't been oblivious to all the female attention he attracted. Women had been staring at him all night, trying to garner his interest. She'd felt a twinge of jealousy, but she'd tamped it down, knowing she had no right to be territorial about Tate. He hadn't belonged to her in a very long time. That had become painfully clear when she'd learned about his relationship with Kit.

"What put that little crinkle in the middle of your forehead?" Tate reached out and smoothed her forehead with his thumb and forefinger, his touch as light as a feather. As always, even the slightest touch from Tate gave rise to an intense longing from somewhere deep in her soul.

"I was just talking to Jenna. She seems so different. Sad. Distant. She barely uttered a few sentences to me before she took off. What's your take on her?"

"Haven't seen her much over the years. She's kind of a recluse if you ask me. I heard she bought a house out by the old Native American graveyard. She lives alone out there and pretty much keeps to herself."

"Does she have a boyfriend?" Cassidy asked.

"Not that I know of. If she does he's the invisible kind," Tate said with a smirk. "In a town this size I would have heard of a boyfriend if he existed."

"She doesn't date?" Cassidy asked, surprised at the

fact that a woman as stunning as Jenna would choose to live such a sheltered life.

Tate shook his head. "Guys have asked her out plenty of times. I know that for sure. But she hasn't taken any of 'em up on their offers. From what I hear she's getting a reputation for being stuck-up. They seem to think she thinks she's better than them."

Cassidy frowned. Jenna wasn't a snob. If anything it had always been the reverse. She'd never felt good enough in West Falls. She'd never felt comfortable in her own skin.

"Dance with me?"

Tate's deep, healing voice washed over her. His offer caught her off guard, instantly taking her mind off Jenna. She crinkled up her nose. "Oh, I get it. You really want to give them something to talk about don't you?" she teased.

Tate grinned and rocked back on his cowboy boots. His eyes twinkled with mischief.

"I've never cared much for what people might say." He leaned down, his smooth cheek brushing against hers as he whispered in her ear. "And the only thing they could say is that the Sheriff was dancing with the most beautiful woman in town."

She felt her cheeks warming with the compliment. "Their tongues are already wagging," she said after casting a quick glance around her. She held out her hand. "Why not?"

Her grabbed her by the hand and whisked her into his arms. His arms were around her waist and they were swaying to the upbeat tempo of Tug Matthews and his band. Cassidy could smell the cool crisp scent of his aftershave. She felt the raw power of his arms as they guided her across the floor. She wished she could capture this moment in a bottle and make it last forever.

When the band stopped for a break, Tate led her off the dance floor, his hand gently entwined with her own. She noticed a few smiles in their direction— her high school math teacher, Cullen Brand, Malachi Finley, Regina—and it made her almost as happy as being with Tate. Nobody was whispering or pointing at her. Nobody seemed put out by her presence at the gathering. A few people had even approached her and thanked her for working so hard on the event. Was it possible that her efforts to restore Main Street Church were helping her win redemption in the eyes of the townsfolk?

Tate took two glasses of sparkling cider from one of the servers and handed one to her.

"I think a toast is in order." He held his glass up in the air. "It's official. Tonight is a resounding success. Main Street Church will have more than enough money in the coffers for a new roof. A few months from now we can focus on restoring the steeple."

Cassidy raised her glass and clinked glasses with Tate. "I don't think I've properly thanked you, Tate, or your family for hosting this at the ranch. Your family really stepped up to support this event. I know that can't have been easy." Although Tate had never discussed his parents' reaction to his offer to host the event at Horseshoe Bend Ranch, she could only imagine that there had been some tense moments and fiery discussions. However it had happened, the end result was the same. The gathering had been wildly successful.

"You're quite welcome, but all we did was provide

the venue," Tate answered in a humble voice. "This all came about because of the congregation working together. I would never have had the imagination to come up with all this." He spread his arms wide. "And without the community supporting it, all our efforts would have been in vain."

"Main Street Church is important to so many people in this town. People need a place to come together, to gather under one roof as a community. There are so many people who draw their strength from being part of a congregation. As far as I'm concerned, that's sacred."

"You never gave up on this town, did you? Or on Holly?" His eyes sparkled with wonder. He reached out and caressed her cheek with his knuckles.

No, she'd never given up. Even in her darkest hours she'd never stopped hoping and dreaming and praying that one day she'd be able to be a part of this town she adored.

"I never gave up on you either," she whispered. "I never could."

His piercing blue eyes seemed to look through her, straight to her very soul. Tate leaned down and brushed a kiss against her forehead, his lips soft and gentle. She closed her eyes and savored that instant, managing to block out everything else going on around her. The kiss spoke to her—of forgiveness and hope and fresh starts. It reminded her of how she'd always felt in Tate's arms—cherished. And if she lived to be a hundred she would never forget this moment, because it was the first time since she'd come back home that she began to hope for new beginnings.

Chapter Ten

"It's time to change out of these party clothes," Cassidy said as Tate led her inside the Lynch home and toward the first floor bathroom. "I need to head over to the kids tent and get started on the art activities."

Although there was something Cinderella-like about Cassidy having to ditch her party duds for an artist's smock, he knew she couldn't have been more jazzed about working with the kids. It was a long-held dream of hers. It didn't escape his notice that she was beaming with pride.

A tent had been set up behind the Lynches' house for children and teenagers from the community. For a nominal sum Cassidy was providing an art lesson, allowing them to experiment with different mediums—water colors, pastels, colored pencils, oils. It was a win-win situation for everyone. If the kids were being entertained at the tent during the event, it increased the likelihood that people would attend the event. They wouldn't have to worry about hiring babysitters or leaving the gathering early due to childcare issues. And it added additional revenue to the proceeds.

So far, tonight had been an evening full of goodwill and revelry. It was one of those nights you wanted to last forever, till all the twinkling stars had been stamped out of the pewter sky.

And he knew how important Cassidy's role in this night had been. Her big heart. Her abiding faith. Her never-ending hope.

"Can I walk you over?" he asked, wanting to be in her presence as much as possible. The thought of not being with her made him ache inside. It was almost a physical pain that left him feeling rattled. What was happening to him?

Her mouth turned upward in a beguiling smile. "I'd like that, Tate. Just give me a few minutes to switch up my clothes."

In five minutes flat she emerged from the bathroom—face scrubbed of makeup, hair swept up in a ponytail, her cute figure dressed in a pair of worn jeans and a plain white T-shirt. She was holding a smock in her hand.

He couldn't help but laugh at her daring. "A white top? For painting with a bunch of kids?"

Cassidy chuckled as they made their way outside. "Hey, there's a method to my madness. I like seeing all the paint and the colors on my shirt. It's a reminder of the creativity and the passion that comes out when you're creating artwork. It'll be as if I'm capturing the joy of the moment on my clothing." She shook her head. "I know that must sound silly."

"It doesn't sound silly at all," he assured her. In fact, it sounded wonderful. He didn't think he'd ever come across anyone who enjoyed their profession as much as she did. The way she felt about art, her excitement and desire to create, moved him deeply. It was said that everyone had a calling in life. Cassidy had tapped into hers as a teenager, and she'd been building on that foundation ever since. He couldn't wait to see her in her element.

Just as they reached the entrance to the tent, Cassidy stopped in her tracks. She looked a bit pale. She clutched at his arm, her eyes wide with concern as she asked, "Tate! What if nobody brought their kids? I mean, what if…I'm not the most popular person in this town. What if nobody wanted me to teach art to their kids?"

He reached out and smoothed back Cassidy's hair, wishing he was bold enough to place a kiss on her lips. *Be patient*, he cautioned himself. *I don't want to scare her away again.*

"Just take a deep breath," he urged her. "You've come this far. Don't stop believing now. I'd never set you up for a fall." He winked at her, watching as she bucked up and strode forward with energy and confidence.

Lord, please lift Cassidy up in this moment. Let her use her special gift to help heal this community. Please allow her to shine as bright as the sun.

Tate pulled back the tent flap and ushered Cassidy inside. He turned toward her, watching her face intently to gauge her reaction. Her mouth swung open and she let out a gasp of surprise. The tent was filled to capacity with children. Children of all ages—toddlers, middle schoolers, tweens—were sitting at tables eating chocolate chip cookies and smores.

Doc Sampson had volunteered to cook on the grill for all the kids taking part in the program, serving a menu of cheeseburgers, hot dogs and fries. With the help of his granddaughter Robin and his staff, he was just now clearing the tables and cleaning up from dinner.

With a stunned expression, Cassidy turned to him, her eyes wide and shocked. "Can you believe this?" she asked Tate. "I never imagined there'd be so many of them." Her eyes once again swept the room and he knew she was letting it all soak in.

This was redemption, Tate thought. Having the town turn out for the community gathering was one thing. But to have all the children eagerly lined up and waiting for her—it was quite another. To have the townsfolk entrust their children to her care was such a leap of faith. He watched Cassidy's face light up, saw the joy shining in her eyes and the heartfelt emotion on her countenance.

She clapped her hands together and let out a loud whistle, immediately capturing the attention of the kids. "Are you guys ready to get dirty?" she shouted. "Because I know I am!"

A dull roar went up, and she playfully covered her ears. The kids were standing up from their benches now and jumping up and down with excitement. Volunteers began handing out smocks, canvases and paintbrushes.

"Okay, everyone. Let's make some excitement," Cassidy said as she began placing paints on each table. She would stop for a few minutes at every table, giving instructions, lending a critical eye or simply watching the kids paint. The kids ate up the attention. Every now and again he would hear one of them cry out, "Miss Cassidy. Look at my painting!" or "Miss Cassidy. I need you."

She was great with kids. Patient. Kind. Loving. She radiated enthusiasm. It made him think of what it would be like to raise a house full of children with her. To wake up on a Saturday morning and make pancakes with Cassidy while their kids finger-painted in the backyard. Teaching their children to ride out at the ranch while Cassidy watched nearby. The images he conjured up seemed so real it made him ache inside. He could picture it all so vividly. A future with Cassidy. Marriage. The white picket fence. The whole nine yards.

But hadn't he told himself hundreds of times that he had no future with her? Hadn't all that crashed and burned years ago? He was no longer so sure of that, no longer certain that he could deny the feelings he'd suppressed for all this time. But what chance did they have when in a little over a month she'd be walking out of his life again?

Instead of heading back to the festivities, he found himself rooted to the spot, unable to take his eyes off Cassidy as she painted with the kids. By the time she made her way back to where he was standing he was ready to burst.

He raised his arm in a sweeping gesture. "You really do have a way with kids. You're amazing." His eyes swept over her—the tousled hair, the paint-spattered shirt, the joyful look on her face. The way she whirled around the room—brushing here, dabbing there, showering the kids with praise—she was like a force of nature.

Cassidy looked back at him, her face radiating warmth and happiness. She looked at ease, not only with herself but with her place in the community. She fit in so effortlessly to the fabric of West Falls. She belonged here. If only he could convince her to stay.

"It feels so natural. They're all so talented and creative," she raved. "They're like little sponges, ready to absorb everything I'm teaching them." Her face was flushed with color, her eyes flashing like emeralds. He'd never seen her look so alive.

"You're really talented, Cass. The way your brush flew over the canvas, creating something so powerful out of nothing. It gave me chills."

Her face lit up with pleasure. "Thanks. I never get tired of hearing that. I feel so blessed to be able to do what I love to do."

"I mean, you were always a great artist, but now... it kind of takes my breath away."

It was that simple. And that nerve-racking.

Tonight wouldn't have been the same without her. Her planning and creativity had pulled it all together. With her oversized heart and her desire to help out, she'd shown how invested she was in Main Street Church. And in doing so, she'd cemented a place for herself within the West Falls community. Ever since the accident people hadn't been able to think of Cassidy without thinking of that evening. Tonight had changed all that.

Creating artwork with the children of West Falls was a dream come true. Just when she'd thought the evening couldn't get any better, she'd ended up on cleanup duty with Regina and Holly. It was a wonder they even got anything done with all the laughing, joking and traipsing down memory lane. Regina had them both in

stitches with her impression of their gym teacher, while
Holly reminded them all of their celebrity crushes.

"Do you remember a certain actor's photo you had
taped in your locker?" she asked, looking pointedly at
Cassidy.

Regina almost choked on her laughter. "She even
had his poster on her bedroom ceiling so he would be
the last thing she saw before she went to bed at night."

"Remember that pink notebook with the hearts?"
Holly asked. "She used to write his name over and over
again in indelible ink." She let out a snort of laughter.

"Stop laughing! It was a very serious relationship. I
was going to marry him and become the wife of a very
famous Hollywood actor." Cassidy stuck her tongue
out in their direction.

Holly and Regina started singing the theme song to
his television show, their voices off-key and cracking.

Cassidy couldn't keep a straight face. She burst out
into giggles. It was strange, she thought, how easily
they'd slipped back into the familiar rhythms of their
friendship. Already they were finishing each other's
sentences and making plans for a girls' night out. Their
camaraderie made her feel wistful about not living in
West Falls. It made her wonder how different her life
might be if she moved back home.

She gathered up a bag of trash and walked it over
to the Dumpster. Maggie was standing there in the
shadows, gazing in the direction of where she'd been
cleaning up with Holly and Regina. Cassidy tensed up,
bracing herself for an unpleasant encounter.

"Watching the three of you took me back aways,"

Maggie said softly. "All you need is Jenna to make it complete."

"I don't think that's going to happen," Cassidy said ruefully. "Jenna doesn't seem interested in reunions. She's kind of a lone wolf now from what I hear."

"Don't give up on her, Cassidy. Sometimes people go through things that the rest of us can't understand. I know what it's like to be in so much pain that you think distancing yourself from the world is the answer." She shook her head, regret stamped all over her face. "All it does is make you lonely."

"I'm not giving up on her, but we're all adults now. If she doesn't want to play in the sandbox with the rest of us, we can't really make her." The moment the words left her mouth, she wanted to pull them back in. She hadn't meant to be rude to Maggie, but it had been a long night and she was bone tired. If Jenna wanted to be standoffish and cold—if keeping her distance truly made her happy—there was nothing Cassidy could do about it. She was done feeling guilty about everything under the sun.

Cassidy tossed the bag into the Dumpster, then wiped her gritty hands on her jeans. "I'm sorry, Maggie. That came out wrong...I didn't mean to be disrespectful."

Maggie cleared her throat. "No worries. Actually I'm the one who owes you an apology for what happened that day out at the stables." She looked down at the ground, her face miserable. "I had no idea you'd already seen Holly, that the two of you had a private meeting at church. Forgive me for opening up old wounds. After all this time nothing can be served by doing that."

She held up her hands to ward off an apology. "You

don't have to apologize. Believe me, I understand where you were coming from." Cassidy paused, filled with uncertainty. She knew it was important to tread lightly with Maggie. "And I just want to let you know, I don't blame you for not giving my letters to Holly."

Maggie's eyes went wide and she began to stammer. "W-what are you talking about?"

"That day at the stables you gave yourself away. When you lit into me you said I'd never called. You never said a word about writing Holly, because you knew I did. Am I right?"

Maggie's jaw trembled. She slowly nodded. Her voice came out as a croak. "Does Holly know?"

"No, although I'm sure she suspects. She thought it was Tate, but I talked her down from that theory. I knew he wouldn't have kept my letters from Holly."

"What you must think of me." Maggie's hand flew to her mouth. Her eyes began to tear up.

Cassidy walked toward Maggie, quickly bridging the distance between the two of them. "I learned a long time ago not to judge people too harshly. It's not fair to measure you by one bad decision. You're a good woman, Maggie and an even better mother. I know you were only trying to protect Holly." She pulled Maggie's hand away from her mouth and entwined it with her own.

Maggie let out a harsh laugh. "I thought by keeping your letters from her I was saving her from more heartache, but the only thing I did was add to her pain." She sniffed back the tears.

Cassidy squeezed her hand. "You have to forgive yourself. Take it from me, you can get wrapped up in the guilt instead of moving forward. What purpose would that serve?"

"There's only one way I can move forward," Maggie asserted. "I need to tell her what I've done and give her the letters." She let out a tortured sigh. "It won't be easy, but I've got to fess up."

Righting wrongs was never easy. But in the end, as Cassidy was certain Maggie would come to understand, it was the only way she'd be able to look herself in the mirror. If she knew Holly the way she thought she did, she'd be furious at first over the deception, but after all was said and done, she'd show her mother compassion.

Cassidy began to pray. She prayed for Maggie and Holly and the entire Lynch family. And she prayed for herself. Because she knew now that she had to tell Tate the truth about the accident. If Maggie could come clean after all these years, then so could she. Maybe not tonight. But soon. Not telling him the truth was tantamount to a lie. And didn't Tate deserve the truth? She'd come so far in the past few months, way too far not to complete the journey. With a sinking heart she realized that in telling him about the accident she might lose him forever.

"Love bears all things, believes all things, hopes all things, endures all things." She hadn't realized she'd been praying aloud until she heard Maggie's melodious voice joining her in prayer.

Hours later when all the guests were gone, the band had broken down their set, the volunteers had helped to clean up the grounds and pack up the tables, Tate and Cassidy were sitting on the front veranda relaxing in the porch swing. Tate had invited her to stay at the ranch for a while so they could both unwind from the exhausting day and evening. With a shy smile, she had agreed.

The weather had cooled down a bit, to the point where Cassidy was shivering in the night air. Without saying a word he removed his jacket and draped it over her shoulders. She wrapped the jacket around herself, snuggling into the fabric.

"I can't believe how quiet it is," she marveled. "Listen. You can hear the crickets chirping. Yet less than a few hours ago this place was jam-packed with people partying for a cause."

"The quiet is nice, isn't it?" He placed his arm around her shoulder, giving in to the desire he'd been fighting against all night. He wanted to hold her, to be near her, to make up for all the time they'd lost. Rather than worry about her leaving, he wanted to focus on the fact that for this one moment in time she was still here beside him.

"It's so peaceful out here," she murmured. "Your family is so blessed to have this ranch. Acres and acres of wide open spaces."

Tate couldn't agree with Cassidy more. In his life he'd been graced with so many blessings. A wonderful family, Horseshoe Bend Ranch, a career in law enforcement…and Cassidy.

"That's for sure. And we're very thankful to my grandfather. He's the one who took a chance and left his home state of Kentucky based on nothing more than gumption and faith." Tate rocked the swing ever so gently with his legs, enjoying the back and forth motion.

"Sounds like someone else I know," she teased, nudging him in the side with her elbow.

"Who, me?" he scoffed, not making the connection between his grandfather and himself.

"Yeah, you. It takes a lot of gumption to be Sheriff of West Falls. And you've always had a lot of faith, not just in God, but in people. I've always loved that about you, Tate."

"Cassidy," he murmured her name. Her face was upturned, her eyes full of wonder. He leaned down and captured her lips in a tender, emotional kiss that left him breathless. As his lips moved over hers he felt her fingers grazing the hair on the back of his neck as she clung to him. He wanted this kiss to go on forever, to lose himself in her. As the kiss ended she breathed his name, making it sound like an endearment.

He brushed his fingers across his lips. He felt so connected to Cassidy at this moment. Was he going crazy? With this kiss he finally felt as if he was home. In that one moment all the pain and heartache of the past eight years had melted away. All that was left was the two of them. Nothing else mattered.

They stared into each other's eyes. He saw a hint of uncertainty lurking there.

"Are you sure about this?" she asked, her brow furrowed.

Tate chuckled. "Are you trying to scare me off or something?"

"No, of course not. It's just that…I know I hurt you before. Terribly. I know there are a lot of wounds here." She reached out and tapped her palm against his chest.

"And when you almost kissed me the night of the storm you talked about regret."

"I'm healing from all that. And a lot of that has to do with your being back in town. It's made me see things with a new set of eyes. It's allowed me to close the door on the past. At the same time I'm looking toward the future."

"I can't promise you—"

He placed a finger on her lips. "Shhh. No promises. Let's just savor the moments."

Cassidy sighed. "I like the sound of that."

"And by the way, Cassidy, I could never regret kissing you. Not in this lifetime."

He'd only spoken of regret because he didn't want to be disappointed. He watched her light up, saw the huge grin stretching from ear to ear. She reached for his hand, joining it with hers in an easy, relaxed manner. He squeezed it tightly, finding comfort in her tiny hand paired with his larger one. For what seemed like forever they sat in the moonlight gazing at the stars, basking in the simple pleasure of each other's company. It was enough. For now. For always.

Chapter Eleven

On her way back home from the oncologist's office with her mother, Cassidy made the suggestion that they stop by an ice cream parlor a few miles outside town. Neither one of them could resist ice cream, nor could they drive past the quaint pink and white shop with the fuschia shutters without stopping inside. It was like something from a fairy tale, Cassidy decided, as she admired the pink heart-shaped tables and the pastel chairs.

"Mmm. This is a decadent way of celebrating," her mother raved as she heartily dug into her ice cream sundae. It pleased Cassidy no end to see her mother's healthy appetite and the way she was making short order of the frozen treat. She was still far too thin for Cassidy's liking.

Cassidy reached over and took a spoonful of her mother's mocha chip ice cream. "Yes, it is, but you deserve a treat after everything you've been through." She shook her head in amazement. "You haven't complained once since I've been here. Not a single time."

"What's there to complain about? God has been good to me, and He's answered all my prayers."

Cassidy smiled at her mother's upbeat frame of mind. "You're really an inspiration, Mama. The way you've stood up to cancer…it's really shown me a lot about who I want to be in the world and how I want to face life's challenges."

Her mother always faced problems head-on without wavering. She used her faith as a foundation and drew strength from God and from within. Cassidy knew she needed to lean on the Lord as the time drew ever nearer for her discussion with Tate. As it was, the secret was wearing on her something fierce, making her feel guilty and shameful whenever she was around him.

"Aren't you meeting up with Tate in an hour or so?"

"Uh-huh. We're meeting at the Falls Diner."

Her mother gave her a curious look. "You don't seem very pressed to get back to town."

She twisted her mouth ruefully. "I'm not sure seeing Tate is a good idea anymore."

Surprise flared in her mother's eyes. "I thought the two of you were enjoying yourselves and getting reacquainted."

"We are," Cassidy acknowledged. "But sometimes I just wonder what the point is. I'm leaving for Phoenix in a few weeks. I just don't want to start something that I can't finish."

Lately the thought of leaving West Falls was weighing heavily on her mind. She'd gotten so used to the laid-back rhythms of her hometown that the thought of the hustle and bustle of Phoenix paled in comparison. And ever since the community gathering, she'd been treated with actual kindness by most of the townsfolk. A few of the parents had even approached her with gratitude about the art class she'd held there. Leaving her hometown this time around wouldn't be easy.

Her mother frowned and pushed her ice cream sundae to the side. "What's really bothering you, Cass? Relationships aren't confined to one zip code. The two of you could easily visit each other and build on that if the feelings are strong enough. You know your father and I would be delighted if you would come back home more often."

Cassidy sighed. "Mom, there's something about the accident that I never told you. Something bad." She waited a beat, watching from across the table as her mother steeled herself. "The night of the accident we were playing chicken with the car…that's why it skidded off the road."

Her mother gasped, then raised her hand to her mouth. Her eyes were wide with shock and disappointment. "Cassidy Anne Blake! Why would you girls ever do something so dangerous?" she asked in a stern voice. "You all could easily have been killed!"

She hung her head, not wanting to even make eye contact with her mother. "We were young and foolish. I can't even wrap my head around how immature we were. We were four teenagers looking for a thrill, I suppose. Never in our wildest dreams did we think something bad would happen."

Her mother tutted. "You girls were always so responsible, such good citizens of your community. Yet I always had the feeling something more went on that night, particularly when all the friendships fell apart afterward, but I never put the pieces together."

"We swore each other to secrecy. Tate doesn't know."

"Oh, dear. And that secret is standing between you and Tate, isn't it?"

Cassidy teared up. She was under so much pressure she felt as if she could explode. "I can't go on like this, Mama. Keeping secrets about something so important isn't who I want to be. I want to be better than that. I know it might cost me Tate, but if I don't tell him then everything we've built will be based on half-truths."

"The path of the righteous is like the first gleam of dawn, shining ever brighter till the full light of day."

Her mother was a true pastor's wife. She had a scripture for every situation under the sun. And this time her scripture touched Cassidy in the deepest regions of her heart. Although she'd known for some time that she owed Tate the truth, she hadn't been able to take that step. Until now. She knew without a shadow of a doubt that she wanted her world to be as radiant as the full light of day.

Just after his shift ended at the Sheriff's Office Tate walked into the Falls Diner, his arms full of a vibrant bouquet of calla lilies, snapdragons and roses. All day he hadn't been able to stop thinking about Cassidy. Her radiant smile mesmerized him. Her joyful spirit always lifted him up. The cute little freckles scattered across her face made him want to kiss her. Her generous heart inspired him to greatness.

She was meeting him here for dinner after finishing up with her mother's weekly oncology appointment. They were celebrating—Main Street Church had a new roof. He'd offered to take her somewhere more fancy, but she'd declined, reminding him that she was a big fan of Doc's cheeseburgers. He looked down at the bouquet of flowers, wondering if they were too over the top. He still didn't know how Cassidy felt about him. He had a hunch she felt the same way he did, but what did he know anyway? He could barely keep his own feelings straight. Something was holding him back from voicing his feelings to her. He couldn't stop the doubt from creeping in, leaving him questioning whether or not they had a future.

Was it wise to try to reignite a flame that had already been extinguished?

And it was difficult to even consider laying his heart on the line when he knew she'd soon be leaving West Falls to go back to her gallery. How could he compete with the life she'd built for herself in Phoenix? Did he even have the gumption to try?

By the time she walked into the diner—fifteen minutes late—he was feeling a bit grumpy and out of sorts. The very sight of her caused him to suck in a deep breath. She looked beautiful in a simple floral skirt and sleeveless top. He stood up when Robin walked Cassidy to the booth he was sitting at, noticing right away the way she avoided eye contact with him and seemed a bit jumpy.

"Is everything okay? I was beginning to think you weren't coming," he said as soon as she got settled in her seat, a slight edge to his voice.

"I'm sorry, Tate," she apologized. "It's been a long day."

"How did your mother make out at her doctor's visit?" He could clearly see the stress and strain on her face and it dawned on him that the checkup might not have gone well.

Cassidy gave him a half smile. "It went amazingly well. Her doctors are very pleased with the scans and her recovery." She let out a sigh that sounded as if it came from deep within her soul.

"If you want to head home, I understand. We can do this some other time."

"No, it's fine. Unless of course you want to head home."

"I'm good if you are," he said, making an effort to hide his dismay. Her indifference caught him off guard, making him question whether he'd been kidding himself.

Robin appeared at their table to take their order. It gave him a chance to study Cassidy while she asked Robin a few questions about an item on the menu. He wasn't sure what was going on, but suddenly they were tripping over each other like two teenagers on their first date. Cassidy wasn't acting like herself. She was skittish and disconnected. Their conversation was nonexistent. The flowers he'd brought her sat beside him in the booth, neglected and unloved. He didn't have the heart to give them to her. It was a grand gesture that didn't seem appropriate given the tension hovering in the air between them.

His heart was all tied up in knots. He couldn't help but feel that he was losing Cassidy all over again, and if he wasn't mistaken, it felt just as painful as the first time.

Fear unlike any she'd ever known held Cassidy in its unrelenting grip. Although she was supposed to be enjoying a dinner date with Tate, she could barely get the food down her throat. Being so close to him and keeping this secret was unbearable. It burned inside her like acid. She didn't want to hurt him all over again. She didn't want to see the pain in his eyes when he discovered the truth. The thought of him hating her was too much to bear.

All through dinner she'd avoided looking into his beautiful eyes, because every time she gazed into them guilt washed over her. The longer she stayed in West Falls the more intensely guilty she felt about withholding the truth from Tate. Once he knew everything he wouldn't even be able to look at her without disgust rising up within him.

Over the previous few weeks they'd managed to lay to rest some of the issues from the past. All of that would disintegrate in a heartbeat. He'd look at her with the same wounded eyes as when he'd first spotted her in the diner. He'd hate her. And the very thought of Tate hating her caused her physical pain.

Tate. The man she loved. The one she didn't think she could live without.

Although she'd known it for a while, she'd stuffed the feelings deep down inside herself, not wanting to recognize them for what they were. It was too scary to be in love with Tate. Hadn't she been down this road before? And she'd hurt him—broken him—to the point where she wasn't sure he would even allow himself to love her again.

She looked down and nervously twiddled her fingers.

Lord, how can I face losing Tate when I just found him again?

"Cassidy! Cassidy!" The sound of his snapping fingers caught her attention. She hadn't heard a word he'd said. She swung her gaze toward Tate, recognizing the hurt look in his eyes.

"Sorry. What did you say?"

"I asked you if you wanted something for dessert. Pie? A milkshake?"

She swallowed past the lump in her throat. "No thanks. I'm stuffed," she said in a quiet voice that hid all the anxiety bubbling up inside her.

"Stuffed? You barely ate half of your meal." Tate's voice sounded incredulous.

Arctic blue eyes studied her and she saw the questions looming in their depths. He'd always been able to read her so well, but tonight she wasn't sending out any signals. It felt as if they were worlds apart. There was still the truth about the accident lying between them and it felt like an insurmountable barrier.

Just as Tate was ridding himself of all the anger and pain, she was now faced with unleashing a world of heartache on him. And knowing Tate as she did, he would react by retreating back into his shell of rage and hurt. All she wanted to do at the moment was bury herself under her covers and hide away from the world, to pretend as if it wasn't her responsibility to tell the truth.

As Tate settled the check, Cassidy studied him from across the table. She wanted to capture the picture of him in her mind so that once she went back to Phoenix she could recall his image at will. There would be many nights ahead when she would think of him just before she closed her eyes and headed off toward a fitful sleep.

His baby blue eyes. The manly cleft in his chin. His

mane of chocolate-colored hair. His broad shoulders that were made to be leaned on.

Losing Tate the first time had been devastating. Losing him a second time might be more than she could bear.

Chapter Twelve

Holly, Regina, Jenna and Cassidy had all gathered at Horseshoe Bend Ranch. A few days earlier Cassidy had laid it all on the line with Holly. She'd told her that she needed to come clean with Tate about the accident— that they couldn't build a relationship on a lie. Holly had been a real friend, listening as she cried her heart out to her and spoke of her dreams for the future. Just like in the old days, Holly had vowed to help her. They had both realized that in order to move forward they had to let the other girls know that they no longer wanted to be bound to their vow of secrecy. After all they'd been through together, it was the only fair thing to do.

Holly had made all the phone calls, and without being explicit, she'd let Regina and Jenna know that this meeting was of the utmost importance. Jenna had balked at meeting up with the three other roses, but Holly had been persistent, making subtle references to "unfinished business."

Jenna was the last to arrive at the ranch. She'd looked mutinous from the moment she'd stepped into the stables, dressed in a yellow rain slicker and boots. A light rain had been falling all afternoon, creating a gloomy atmosphere at the ranch. Cassidy wrapped her arms around her middle, wishing she'd added another layer to her sweater to ward off the chill in the air.

"What is this all about?" Jenna asked as soon as she walked in, her face twisted in a frown.

"You were very secretive on the phone, Holly," Regina added.

Holly positioned her wheelchair so that all the girls were in view. "Well, Cassidy and I…we don't want to keep the vow anymore. We want to be open and honest about what really happened the night of the crash."

Jenna let out a shocked gasp. "No! We all promised we would never tell."

"We were kids then, Jenna," Cassidy pointed out. "I don't think we had any idea of what keeping a secret like that would entail."

"We've been doing fine all these years," Jenna snapped. "Then suddenly Cassidy comes back to town and wants to turn everything upside down. It's not fair!"

"Fair? Do you really want to talk about fair?" Regina scolded. "Cassidy bore the brunt of everything, Jenna. She was the one who had everything to lose by keeping that vow. It was her reputation that got shredded, not ours."

"When I agreed to keep the secret I was lying in hospital bed with a shattered spine. I think I would've agreed to anything," Holly asserted. She hung her head. "It makes me sick that I've accepted all this sympathy over the years, all the while I've been lying about what really happened."

"Don't you see, Jenna? We've all moved forward to

a point in our lives where the secret is doing more harm than good," Cassidy explained. Jenna was acting as if this was a personal attack on her, when in reality it was unloading a secret that was weighing them all down.

Jenna stayed silent. She stared at them with big, rounded eyes that begged them not to go back on their vow. Cassidy recognized fear when she saw it. She'd lived with it for too long not to know it like the back of her hand. Jenna wasn't just being ornery. She was scared to death.

Cassidy moved forward so that she was in Jenna's direct line of sight. Compassion flowed through her as she saw her lips trembling and the lost look in her eyes.

"I was playing chicken with the car the night of the crash. There's no way I can pretty that up or change it. I have to own it. But we all have some ownership. Even you, Jenna. And like it or not, I can't let my future be dragged down by the past." She shook her head vehemently. "Not anymore. Not ever again."

Tate was stumped. He'd come back to the ranch much earlier than expected after getting off his shift prematurely, only to discover that Holly was nowhere to be found. His parents were out of town looking at purebred horses, so he knew she wasn't with them. He was a little bit concerned, since driving was a new accomplishment for Holly and she might not have the skills to drive in the rain. Plus, it wasn't like her to take off from the ranch without leaving a note or telling the family beforehand.

There was a slight chance she might have driven out somewhere on the property, he thought, as he grabbed his keys and headed for his truck. As he drove past the stables he came across not only Holly's van, but Cassidy's baby blue Honda. When he hopped out of his truck he noticed two other cars—a BMW that looked like the one Regina owned and another car he didn't recognize.

What was Cassidy doing out here? He'd asked her if she wanted to catch a movie tonight, but she'd declined, saying she had plans with her family. With free time on his hands he'd done a shift at the Sheriff's Office instead. Why would all the girls be out here at the stables at nine o'clock at night? He slipped in through the side door, the sound of raised voices emanating from the front of the building.

He could see them all from where he was standing in the shadows. Cassidy. Holly. Regina. And Jenna. The four roses. They seemed to be arguing, he realized. Jenna was flailing her arms and Regina was teary eyed. Cassidy had her arms folded around her chest. Holly seemed agitated.

I was playing chicken with the car the night of the crash. Cassidy's words rang out in the stables. Everything else faded away. He felt blood rushing to his head.

An avalanche of emotion rained down on him. His chest tightened and pain rocketed through him with the force of a sledgehammer. He couldn't remember the last time he'd been this fired up. It felt as if he was on the verge of exploding. He would never have believed it for a second, but he'd heard it with his own ears. Cassidy had outright admitted it. Playing a dangerous game of chicken had caused the accident that had shattered Holly's world. *And my world, as well,* he thought angrily. Cassidy had made decisions the night of the crash that had altered the course of his life. Had he meant so little to her that she'd been willing to toss their future aside for a reckless game?

My sister is in a wheelchair because of some stupid, ridiculous stunt?

He stumbled out of the stables without making a sound. His heart felt as if it were breaking in two. It was actual physical pain that gripped him. He hadn't felt this way since the day he'd found out Cassidy had left town. Betrayal. The sting of it seared his insides.

The rain flowed over him and he did nothing to shield himself. They were cleansing rains that he prayed would soothe his raging soul. There were so many conflicting emotions swirling around inside him. *After everything they'd been through, how could she have kept this from him? What kind of person played games with other peoples lives?* He walked toward his truck, wanting to get as far away from this place as possible.

How could she have lied to him? What a fool he'd been to think that she had changed one iota from the person she'd been eight years ago. Feeling the need to vent some frustration, he kicked the tire on his truck. It did absolutely nothing to ease his agony. What he really wanted to do was scream at the top of his lungs, to have a very noisy conversation with God about the path he'd been walking on. For the past few weeks he'd been more and more certain that the path was leading toward a future with Cassidy. But now, after what he'd just overheard, he couldn't imagine holding her in his arms without thinking about all the lies and evasions.

How could he have been such a fool twice in one lifetime?

With a groan he turned around and walked back in the direction of the stables. He paced back and forth in the rain as memories washed over him. Seeing Cassidy at the diner on her first day back in town. Hanging out with her at Horseshoe Bend Ranch during the storm. Dancing with her at the community gathering.

Could he really have been so wrong about Cassidy?

Every time he turned around to get in his truck and leave, he found himself rooted to the spot. Why was it so hard to walk away from her? Why did the thought of it hurt so badly?

Are you trying to tell me something, Lord? 'Cause if you are, I'm struggling to get the message.

There was no way he could build a life with someone who harbored secrets. It was that simple. Trust was the very foundation of a relationship, yet Cassidy had shattered his faith in her not once, but twice. There were only so many times a person could turn the other cheek.

For a moment everything got real still and he began to pray. *Lord, I love this woman. Regardless of what happened in the past, she is my future. She's my other half, Lord. The other piece of my soul.*

How in the world could he even think of walking away from that?

She'd changed him. Inspired him. She made him want to be a better man, one who didn't struggle with forgiveness but granted it. They'd held hands and prayed together. She'd helped Holly achieve a measure of peace. Together they'd brought Picasso into the world. No one could ever make him laugh the way Cassidy did. And even though she'd been given a hard time since she'd come back to West Falls, she'd stayed.

Suddenly, like a balloon deflating, he felt all the anger leave him.

Forgiveness. He'd reached a state of grace where he could honestly say that he'd forgiven Cassidy for all the pain and heartache she'd caused in the past. How could he turn his back on that? How could he lose her a second time? It would be like losing a limb. He needed her. And he didn't want to live without her. He'd done that before and it had nearly killed him.

No matter what she'd done in the past, he couldn't turn his back on her. It just wasn't possible.

Soaked to the bone, he walked back inside the stables. This time he wasn't hiding in the shadows.

Cassidy winced as the pain seared through her in wave after wave. All she could think about was Tate. When she told him the truth about the accident he wouldn't want anything more to do with her. By withholding the truth, she'd lied to him. It was so clear to her now. She wondered why she hadn't always seen it so clearly.

Lord, please give me the grace to be honest with Tate, regardless of the consequences. And whatever he decides, please give me the strength to get through this.

The debate among the girls was still raging on, but part of her had mentally checked out. She'd already reached a decision about telling Tate the truth. Nothing was going to change that, not even the dread coursing through her veins.

"We were all responsible. All four of us," Holly declared. "But Cassidy took the blame for everything.

All the hatred, the responsibility, the law enforcement interrogation."

"Holly, what are you saying?" Jenna's voice was shrill. "Are you letting her off the hook?"

"That's not what she's saying!" Regina shouted, her voice filled with frustration.

"We all did it! That's what I'm saying. We all played that stupid game," Holly said in a firm voice. "We called it chicken, didn't we? We'd each take turns getting behind the wheel and we'd drive well past the speed limit and act crazy."

"I never drove. I didn't even have my license!" Jenna protested.

"You didn't drive, but you participated. We all did," Regina said, tears shimmering in her eyes. "Not one of us ever said no. Holly's right. We were all responsible."

"Cassidy may have been the one driving the car when the accident happened, but the rest of us all took turns that night. It was just Cassidy's misfortune that she skidded in the rain."

Regina nodded. "It could have been any of us. I know I wasn't a very good driver." She let out a painful laugh. "At seventeen, who is?"

"I didn't have my seat belt on because I was hanging out my window. How stupid was that?" Holly banged her fists on her legs. "If I'd been wearing it, I wouldn't be in this chair."

"We promised we would never talk about this!" Jenna cried. "I don't want to remember that night!"

"I have to talk about this! It's been eating me up inside all this time!" Holly spit out. "For years I've been hiding this, afraid of what everyone would think of us if they found out. But it came at a price. And Cassidy's had to pay that price all by herself."

"We thought we were invincible," Cassidy said with a bitter laugh. "I know I did. Bad things never happened to girls like us, right?"

"Right," Holly said with a shake of her head. "But something bad did happen, didn't it? And I don't think we should let this vow hold us back anymore. As long as we're keeping secrets, we're still stuck in the past."

The sound of footsteps echoed in the stillness of the stables. Cassidy whipped her head around, shock coursing through her as she saw Tate emerging from the shadows.

Tate moved out of the darkness, making his presence known to all the girls. Someone let out a gasp. He heard Cassidy call out his name. All of their attention was now focused on him.

"I need to talk to Cassidy," he fumed. "You all need to leave us alone."

He could barely look at them, didn't want to lash out at them in his current state of fury. He'd heard enough of their conversation to know that Cassidy hadn't been alone in her actions. All of the girls had been part of the game, although none had been brave enough to come clean at the time.

He was so angry at the way they'd hidden the truth. They'd placed the entire burden on Cassidy's shoulders, and she'd suffered for it over the years. She'd lost everything. If they'd banded together and supported her, perhaps she would have been strong enough to stay in West Falls. Perhaps their foolish actions could have served as a cautionary tale for all the teenagers who texted while driving or treated their cars as a right rather than a privilege.

At the harsh sound of his voice, Jenna quickly scrambled away from the stables. Regina cast a sorrowful glance at her cousin, then slowly walked toward the door. Holly wheeled over to him, her expression mutinous as she confronted him.

"Don't let what you overheard change how you feel. Please, Tate. What you and Cassidy have, it's one in a million." Her blue eyes were beseeching him to tread lightly with Cassidy's heart.

"Please," he barked, his anger rising by the second. "I just want to talk to Cassidy."

Surprise flared in Holly's eyes. He had never talked to her this way, but he was so disappointed over what she'd done that he could barely look at her. He didn't want to be civil. There would be time later for the two of them to talk it out. But now, all he wanted was Cassidy.

Please Lord, give me the courage to tell Cassidy how I truly feel about her.

It wasn't easy laying himself bare to her. Making himself vulnerable scared him. It brought back all the nightmarish memories from when he'd lost her. The thought of falling on his face terrified him, but, if there was a chance she felt the same way he did, he would risk it all.

Cassidy's eyes were wide with fear. "How much did you hear?" Her voice sounded raw.

"Everything." There were no more secrets between them. Not now. Not ever, he hoped.

One look in Cassidy's eyes told him everything. Hurt, regret, pain, fear.

Cassidy covered her face with her hands. "I'm so sorry." Her voice was filled with remorse.

"Why didn't you tell me?" All the agony he felt came out in his voice.

"It wouldn't have changed anything," she said, blinking back tears. "And we vowed never to tell, never to speak of it. I didn't want to drag all the other girls down with me."

His frustration bubbled over. "It would have changed everything! Everyone blamed you—"

"Because I was driving when the car skidded off the road."

He reached out and grabbed her by the shoulders, wanting to gently shake some sense into her. Was she still shouldering all the blame? She couldn't possibly think she owned this all by herself.

"But you weren't the only one driving that night. You all took turns, except for Jenna. You were all part of it."

"Ultimately, it was still my fault. I participated in that stupid game. I was at the wheel and I ran my car off the road. Tate, I've had to accept responsibility for my actions. It's the only way I could move forward. It was the only way I could forgive myself."

He reached for her, cupping her face in his hands so he could look into her wounded eyes. More than anything he wanted to nurture her, to shelter her from having to face anything else in life all alone.

"You lost so much that night. I'm not sure you've ever acknowledged what it cost you. Your entire life turned on a dime that night."

"None of us were unscathed," Cassidy pointed out. "Jenna…she's different now. Hardened. And Regina… she's more of a loner, kind of closed off. And Holly. What hasn't she been through with her recovery? There's so much that will forever be out of her reach."

Tate pulled her to him, his lips moving over hers in the purest of kisses. He wanted to show her all the things he'd been afraid to show her before tonight. He wanted to lay it all on the line for her, in the hopes that she saw a future with him. He wanted to give her everything. And above all, forgiveness. As the kiss ended, Cassidy clung to him, whispering words poignant enough to melt his heart.

"Please, forgive me, Tate. For not telling you, for keeping secrets. I don't want to lose you."

Her heart was all tied up in her words. He could see it now and the beauty of it almost brought him to his knees. It flowed over him like healing waters, giving him the courage to say what was in his heart.

"Cass, I know this has been a long time coming, but I forgive you. I don't want the past to ever come between us again. A life without you—" He shuddered. "That's not a life I want to live. Been there, done that. It was a much emptier life without you in it. I love you, Cassidy."

His voice was filled with conviction and he wanted it to heal her, to lift her up to a place where she only saw their bright future. He placed his hands on either side of her face, his thumbs grazing her cheeks.

"I've been prideful. Unyielding. I was so stuck in the past that I couldn't see the future. I've been all over the place with my emotions. I don't know why you even put up with me," he said with an agonized groan.

"Shhh." Cassidy placed her finger over his mouth. "You're the kindest, most tender man I've ever known. I gave you every reason to harden your heart to me. If I haven't said it before, I'm very grateful to be given a second chance to love you. Because I do love you, Tate Lynch. I have fallen madly, deeply, forever in love with you."

He rained kisses down on her face...her nose, cheeks, forehead...dozens of feather-light kisses. She felt like each kiss was removing a scar from her heart. He was healing her with his love. He was showing her that the past wasn't nearly as important as their present.

"I know you have a life in Phoenix, but I'd like you to consider moving back home. I truly believe God led you home to me." Tate's eyes were full of hope.

"I want to come back home. I want to come back to you and my family. And Holly. West Falls is where my heart is...and I can run my gallery from anywhere." Even in the pulsing heartbeat of her hometown. "Oh, and Tate, I can teach art to the kids in the congregation. Weekly classes held at Main Street Church. Can't you just picture it?"

Tate grinned wide and it looked like his heart was filled to overflowing.

She laid her head on his chest, seeking the soft place to fall that only he could provide. He wrapped his large arms around her, surrounding her with a cocoon of love. In the past few months her life had come full circle.

She'd found love again with the only man she'd truly ever loved. And by some miracle this love was stronger, wiser, more grounded. It had been built on a foundation of forgiveness. Her heart had stretched out bigger and wider than she'd ever dreamt possible. Because of him.

Love. Security. Home. A soft place to fall. It was all right here in West Falls with Tate.

Epilogue

Horseshoe Bend Ranch

Cassidy increased her speed to a gallop as she rode in on Fiddlesticks, reaching the stables a hairsbreadth behind Tate, who was riding a white Arabian horse his father had just acquired. She lovingly patted Fiddlesticks, reaching into her shirt pocket for a bag of sliced apples. For weeks now she'd been riding her a few times a week, so much so that she was starting to develop a real attachment to the gentle horse. Even Tate referred to the onyx Arabian as "her horse."

One month ago she'd set up a small gallery on Main Street. She'd decided to run her Phoenix gallery from here in West Falls with the help of her assistant. Her mother's continued good health was the biggest blessing of all. From this point forward she would have to be vigilant about checkups in the event of a recurrence. Although she wouldn't be out of the woods until she was cancer-free for five years, the doctors were optimistic about her prognosis.

Tate had quickly dismounted and was now standing

next to Fiddlesticks, ready to help Cassidy dismount. She freed her feet from the stirrups and swung her leg over Fiddlesticks's rump. Tate held his hands up and caught her in his arms, gently depositing her back on solid ground. Malachi came out of nowhere and took the reins of the horses. With a sly grin in Tate's direction, he led the horses into the stables.

"Malachi is really going to have to stop bending your ear so much, Tate. It's getting to be a real problem," Cassidy quipped. In the past four months she'd only heard Malachi utter a few words at the most. He continued to be an enigma.

"He's the strong silent type," Tate said with a grin. "And as trustworthy as they come."

When she rounded the corner of the stables she stopped in her tracks, taken aback by the sight that greeted her. A picturesque table lit with lanterns had been set up for two. Roses were laid out on the table, along with scattered chocolates and crystal flutes. Joy filled her heart as she realized that Tate had arranged this romantic surprise for her. She whirled around to face Tate, who was sporting a devilish grin.

"When did you do this? Tate, it's so romantic," she gushed, her hand pressed against her heart.

"I had a little help from Malachi. He helped set this up while we were riding," Tate admitted. "C'mon and sit down."

Tate led Cassidy to the table, pulling out the seat for her. She looked around curiously, wondering if the food was nearby. She was actually starving after riding for so long. Tate continued to stand there gazing at her instead of joining her at the table. He opened his mouth a couple times, then closed it. He took off his cowboy hat and raked his hand through his chocolate-brown hair. Two seconds later he was fiddling with his collar and readjusting his cowboy hat.

"Tate, is everything all right?" She didn't know what was going on with him. Was he trying to break some bad news or something?

A huge grin took over his face. He seemed to relax. "All right? Yes, I'm all right. More than all right, actually. I'm happier than I've ever been. That's because of you, Cass."

"We both know we've been down this road before," he continued. "Difference is, we're older and wiser now. We know what it feels like to not have your other half. We know what it's like to love someone, yet not be able to be with that person. We know what it's like to have regret." He swatted away the tears rolling down his face. "I've learned a lot over the past few years. I think I'm a better man. I'm stronger in my faith now. I know that when times get tough I need to lean on the Lord. And more than anything I know what I want for the future." He took a big shuddering breath. "I want you, Cassidy. I want to love you and be loved by you. I want to wake up every morning with you by my side, knowing that no matter what else happens we have each other."

Tate reached into his pocket and pulled out a blue velvet box. He flipped the box open, revealing the antique engagement ring that had been in his family for generations. It sparkled and winked at her, reminding her of the past yet hinting of a glorious future that awaited her. He got down on one knee and took off his cowboy hat, pressing it against his chest as he held the ring up to her.

In a voice husky with emotion, he asked, "Cassidy,

will you marry me? Will you be my partner, my soul mate, my other half…for the rest of our lives?"

Tears of joy spilled down her cheeks and she walked toward him, ending up falling to her knees beside him. She wanted to be looking into his sky-blue eyes when she gave him her answer.

"Yes, I'll marry you, Tate." She gazed into his eyes, seeing her love for him reflected there. At that very moment she kissed him, her lips moving over his in a triumphant, sublime kiss that celebrated everything they'd been through that had brought them to this moment. He brushed his lips over hers, his kiss filled with the promise of forever.

* * * * *

Dear Reader,

I hope you enjoyed visiting West Falls, Texas, and the love story of Cassidy and Tate. I love reunion romances set in small, cozy towns. There's something comforting to me about two people who share a love that withstands the test of time. Cassidy Blake carries around a great deal of guilt and shame due to the accident. She yearns to make amends to all the people who were affected by her actions, particularly Holly and Tate. Throughout her journey toward redemption she turns to God for comfort and strength.

Being part of the Love Inspired family is a dream come true. I can't think of a better job than writing happy endings and working in my pajamas.

Thank you for reading *Reunited with the Sheriff.* I'd love to hear from you. I can be reached at scalhoune@gmail.com. Please visit my website, bellecalhoune.com, to find out about future projects and giveaways.

Warm wishes,
Belle Calhoune

Questions for Discussion

1. Can you understand why Cassidy has avoided coming back home for eight long years? Have you ever avoided a situation and then been forced to confront it?

2. Cassidy's motivation for coming home is her mother's illness. Have you ever been faced with caring for a loved one during a serious illness? How did you deal with it?

3. Tate is pretty hard on Cassidy when he first sees her at the diner. Do you think his actions are justified? Why or why not?

4. Do you think Tate has mixed reasons for being angry at Cassidy? What are some of the reasons? In what ways is his anger holding him back from moving forward?

5. Cassidy's goal is to make amends for all the harm she caused eight years ago, particularly to Holly and Tate. Do you think her goal is realistic? Have you ever sought redemption?

6. When Cassidy attends the church bazaar she is treated poorly by some of the townsfolk. Are their actions understandable? What would you do if you witnessed someone being treated this way?

7. Why do you think Tate turns away from Cassidy at the church bazaar? What emotions is he struggling with in this scene?

8. Holly's injuries in the accident were shattering and permanent, yet she seems to have reached a state of grace where she can forgive Cassidy. What strengths does Holly draw on in order to forgive Cassidy? Do you think you could forgive if you were in Holly's position?

9. Both Cassidy and Holly had moments after the accident where they felt that God had forsaken them. Have you ever been in a place where you felt that God turned His back on you? Have you ever experienced a time when you were angry with God? If so, how did you work through it?

10. Returning Tate's engagement ring is a very emotional experience for both Cassidy and Tate. What does the ring represent for each of them? Was giving the ring back the right thing to do? Why or why not?

11. Maggie Lynch is still furious at Cassidy due to the accident that left her daughter paralyzed. Do you think her actions are in keeping with what the Bible teaches us about forgiveness?

12. When the storm damages Main Street Church the congregation bands together for the purpose of restoring the roof and steeple. In your life have there been instances where your church community banded together for a cause? How do you feel this strengthens a congregation?

13. Do the four roses bear equal responsibility for the accident? What could each of them have done that night to prevent the accident?

14. Were you surprised that Tate forgives Cassidy when the circumstances of the accident are revealed? What allows him to forgive her? At what point does Cassidy realize that she has to forgive herself?

15. The theme of this book is forgiveness and redemption. Have you ever sought forgiveness for a transgression? How did you go about making amends?

REQUEST YOUR FREE BOOKS!

2 FREE INSPIRATIONAL NOVELS
PLUS 2
FREE
MYSTERY GIFTS

Love Inspired

YES! Please send me 2 FREE Love Inspired® novels and my 2 FREE mystery gifts (gifts are worth about $10). After receiving them, if I don't wish to receive any more books, I can return the shipping statement marked "cancel." If I don't cancel, I will receive 6 brand-new novels every month and be billed just $4.74 per book in the U.S. or $5.24 per book in Canada. That's a saving of at least 21% off the cover price. It's quite a bargain! Shipping and handling is just 50¢ per book in the U.S. and 75¢ per book in Canada.* I understand that accepting the 2 free books and gifts places me under no obligation to buy anything. I can always return a shipment and cancel at any time. Even if I never buy another book, the two free books and gifts are mine to keep forever.

105/305 IDN F47Y

Name _____ (PLEASE PRINT) _____

Address _____ Apt. # _____

City _____ State/Prov. _____ Zip/Postal Code _____

Signature (if under 18, a parent or guardian must sign)

Mail to the **Harlequin® Reader Service:**
IN U.S.A.: P.O. Box 1867, Buffalo, NY 14240-1867
IN CANADA: P.O. Box 609, Fort Erie, Ontario L2A 5X3

**Are you a subscriber to Love Inspired books
and want to receive the larger-print edition?
Call 1-800-873-8635 or visit www.ReaderService.com.**

* Terms and prices subject to change without notice. Prices do not include applicable taxes. Sales tax applicable in N.Y. Canadian residents will be charged applicable taxes. Offer not valid in Quebec. This offer is limited to one order per household. Not valid for current subscribers to Love Inspired books. All orders subject to credit approval. Credit or debit balances in a customer's account(s) may be offset by any other outstanding balance owed by or to the customer. Please allow 4 to 6 weeks for delivery. Offer available while quantities last.

Your Privacy—The Harlequin® Reader Service is committed to protecting your privacy. Our Privacy Policy is available online at www.ReaderService.com or upon request from the Harlequin Reader Service.

We make a portion of our mailing list available to reputable third parties that offer products we believe may interest you. If you prefer that we not exchange your name with third parties, or if you wish to clarify or modify your communication preferences, please visit us at www.ReaderService.com/consumerschoice or write to us at Harlequin Reader Service Preference Service, P.O. Box 9062, Buffalo, NY 14269. Include your complete name and address.

LI13R

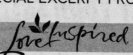
The pavement outside the Kansas City airport radiated heat even though the sun had already sunk below the horizon. Tate held his seven-year-old daughter's hand a little tighter and squinted against the dying sunshine to read the signs hanging overhead.

"That's it down there," he said, pointing. "Baggage Claim A."

Lily Farnsworth was the last of six new business owners to arrive, each selected by the Save Our Street Committee of the town of Bygones. As a member of the committee, Tate had been asked to meet her at the airport in Kansas City and transport her to Bygones. With the grand opening just a week away, most of the shop owners had been at work preparing their stores for some time already, but Ms. Farnsworth had delayed until after her sister's wedding, assuring the committee that a florist's shop required less preparation than some retail businesses. Tate hoped she was right.

He still wasn't convinced that this scheme, financed by a mysterious, anonymous donor, would work, but if something didn't revive the financial fortunes of Bygones—and soon—their small town would become just another ghost town on the north central plains.

Isabella stopped before the automatic doors and waited

for him to catch up. They entered the cool building together. A pair of gleaming luggage carousels occupied the open space, both vacant. A few people milled about. Among them was a tall, pretty woman with long blond hair and round tortoiseshell glasses. She was perched atop a veritable mountain of luggage. She wore black ballet slippers and white knit leggings beneath a gossamery blue dress with fluttery sleeves and hems. Her very long hair was parted in the middle and waved about her face and shoulders. He felt the insane urge to look more closely behind the lenses of her glasses, but of course he would not.

He turned away, the better to resist the urge to stare, and scanned the building for anyone who might be his florist.

One by one, the possibilities faded away. Finally Isabella gave him that look that said, "Dad, you're being a goof again." She slipped her little hand into his, and he sighed inwardly. Turning, he walked the few yards to the luggage mountain and swept off his straw cowboy hat.

"Are you Lily Farnsworth?"

To find out if Bygones can turn itself around,
pick up LOVE IN BLOOM
wherever Love Inspired books are sold.